THE BOOK OF SANA'A

First published in Great Britain in 2025 by Comma Press.
www.commapress.co.uk

'The General Secretariat for Speed Bumps' by Hayel al-Mathabi was first published
in Arabic in the collection, *A City of Wax* (Horouk Manthura, 2015). 'Borrowing
a Head' by Abdoo Taj won first place in the al-Rabadi Award for Short Stories for
2022/2023.

A CIP catalogue record of this book is available from the British Library.

ISBN-10: 1912697971
ISBN-13: 978-1912697977

The publisher gratefully acknowledges the support of Arts Council England.

Supported using public funding by
**ARTS COUNCIL
ENGLAND**

Printed and bound in England by Clays Ltd, Elcograf S.p.A

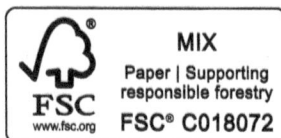

MIX
Paper | Supporting
responsible forestry
FSC® C018072

THE BOOK
OF
SANA'A

EDITED BY
LAURA KASINOF

Contents

CONTENTS

Introduction

THE WEATHER IN SANA'A is unlike any other city in the Arab world. At 2,200 metres above sea level, the air in the Yemeni capital is often crisp like a cool autumn day, brimming with energy and possibility. Nights stay chilly year round and a rainy season drenches Sana'a each summer. Rarely, but sometimes, it even snows in the high desert mountains that surround the city. This all feels anathema to the rest of the Arabian Gulf, which Yemen may be geographically a part of, yet is politically very distant from. Yemen's differences from its neighbours are many and varied – including its recent history housing a republic-style government, as well as its abject poverty.

Near the centre of Sana'a sits its iconic old city, a UNESCO world heritage site where thousands of narrow, multi-storey houses made from ochre-coloured rammed earth, gypsum, and accented with stained glass windows, cram together to create the illusion of a small city of 'gingerbread houses'. Tiny alleyways weave throughout, leading to busy markets, hidden hammams, as well as to the Great Mosque of Sana'a, said to date back to the time of the Prophet Mohammed, and to Soq al-Milh, where each evening men sit at long shared tables to dine on kebab spiced with cumin and chilli.

After dinner, the old city's daily bustle turns to a muted calm. Its alleys shine a golden amber from the occasional streetlamp and the staccato shouts of Sana'ani Arabic become more infrequent until an eerie silence descends over this ancient walled city where people have lived for over two millennia. At night, it becomes easier to remember that, despite the friendly faces behind each stall or the easy charm of old men with canes sipping milky tea in every alleyway, despite the helpful hand so often extended to strangers, this is also an old city filled with prying eyes and families that don't forget, with alliances and enemy lines that run deep and branch off into the countryside where hostility turns violent.

Though no longer the functional centre of Sana'a, the old city is still the spiritual heart of the capital, and Yemenis from across the country regard the old city with a special fondness – despite increasingly divisive politics nationwide that may pit the old city's denizens against their fellow countrymen. Old Sana'a's inhabitants are considered more traditional than the rest of the capital's population, more like villagers whose families have lived in their small block of the old town for hundreds of years. They also tend to be closer aligned with the former, late president of Yemen, Ali Abdullah Saleh (who ruled from 1978 to 2012), or more often now, with the Houthi rebel movement[1] that rules the capital. They are considered original Sana'anis, even though the city has since expanded to contain so much more.

Just outside Sana'a's old city runs a ring road, the *saila*, which becomes packed full of cars each afternoon as Sana'anis leave work around 12pm – the typical end of the work day – to rush home for lunch, with a probable stop at the qat market on the way. The saila is cut deep into the earth, and collects water during the rainy season, acting as a drainage system for the city. During a rainy day, as the saila fills, drivers push their luck to the very last moment, trying to use this shortcut despite rising water levels. In downpours, the saila transforms into a rushing river, young boys dive off bridges into its murky depths, much to the delight of onlookers cheering them on.

From there, Sana'a sprawls out in all directions, to commercial districts of small electronic shops, to offices and grocery stores, to middle-class neighbourhoods of small concrete apartments where people have struggled to make ends meet in recent years. To the south, sits a wealthy neighbourhood of large walled homes and gardens, coffee shops and hamburger joints. Along these roads, beggars from the countryside weave in and out of traffic, hoping to sell jasmine flower necklaces to passing cars.

Nearby, a grand mosque, the largest in Yemen with a capacity for some 40,000 worshippers, and built by President Saleh's regime, stands tall, Sana'a's most notable landmark other than the old city. Its cream and coral colours are a striking palette against the desert mountains surrounding the capital. In front of the mosque runs a large thoroughfare, 70th Street, often used for showy military parades and fiery political protests.

'All the devils are in Sana'a,' I remember a tribal leader telling me when I used to live in the city, now some fifteen years ago. Though I don't remember who exactly told me this, I can picture the room where I heard it. We were chewing qat, reclining on the low cushions of a diwan (traditional Yemeni reception room), a staple in any northern Yemen home. Likewise, the words have stayed with me. The sheikh had meant that everyone from across the country who had any real social or political power, often wielded for self-gain at any cost, had come to Sana'a, bringing their problems with them. These days, Sana'a is less cosmopolitan, more homogenous politically, as the Houthis' political foes have fled south, or out of Yemen altogether. Though some of the 'devils' remain.

In the fall of 2014, the tides of Yemen shifted drastically when the Houthi rebels seized Sana'a, with the aid of former President Saleh, who was then assassinated a few years later by the same rebels he had helped empower. Since 2014, Yemen has been divided, the Houthis controlling the 'North' from Sana'a, and the remnants of Yemen's previous republic-style government in Aden in the 'South',[2] redrawing some of the old lines of a country that had long been divided prior to unification under President Saleh in 1990.[3]

Sana'a has also been the site of much bloodshed. A Saudi

Arabia-led military coalition at war with the Iran-backed Houthis has bombed much of northern Yemen, Sana'a included. Even the beloved old city has been hit. Scores have been killed in Saudi's bombing campaign and many more Yemenis have died as a result of a blockade Saudi has enforced on the north. In 2024, Sana'a was pulled into the wider war in the Middle East as Israel's genocidal war on Gaza has spilled out into a larger regional conflict. In retaliation for Houthi attacks on Red Sea shipping and drones sent toward Tel Aviv, the United States and United Kingdom have bombed Houthi targets inside Yemen.

Meanwhile, under Houthi leadership, freedom of expression, which Yemenis used to enjoy relative to other dictatorships in the Arab world, has been erased. Activists, journalists and writers are languishing in prison in Sana'a. (And notably, press freedom has declined in recent years in southern Yemen as well, which is ruled, at least on paper, by the internationally-recognised Yemeni government.)

During the 33-year-long Saleh regime, Yemeni writers could mostly write as they pleased, except in a few specific cases when a writer or journalist would get under Saleh's skin and the former president would go after the writer with a personal vendetta, sometimes with fatal consequences. These cases were terrible, and it was difficult to know where Saleh would draw his red lines, but still Yemen had a somewhat functioning press. That is no longer the case, which is why it is even more remarkable to publish this book celebrating writing coming out of Sana'a.

When it comes to the larger Arab world, especially with regard to art and culture, Yemen is often overlooked. Yet the country, and Sana'a specifically, has a long literary history where politics and writing frequently have overlapped. In the mid-20th century, among the revolutionaries who worked to overthrow the imamate which had ruled northern Yemen until 1962, was the well-known poet, novelist and Sana'ani, Muhammad Mahmoud al-Zubairi. He was later exiled, then returned, and then assassinated, and now has a major thoroughfare named after him in Sana'a.

The Book of Sana'a introduces readers to this world of Yemeni writing through more established novelists like Badr Ahmed, and Hayel al-Mathabi, burgeoning Yemeni women writers, like Maysoon al-Eryani and Rim Mugahed, and writers for whom this is among their first fiction published, like Afaf al-Qubati. The stories in this book range from political satire, to a meditation on mother-daughter relationships, to a story of a family of jinn residing in Sana'a's old city. For many of the stories, political upheaval and war provide a backdrop to life; for instance, in Badr Ahmed's story, we see the Saleh regime's violent crackdown on Sana'a's Arab Spring protests. And throughout, a bit of Sana'a's history, its heart and soul, spills out onto the pages, offering a snapshot of a city that is becoming increasingly shut off from the outside world.

When I was fortunate enough to live in Sana'a, the city would often pull me to attention, as if it reached out and grabbed me. I would find myself sitting in the back seat of a random taxi, deep in thought about the kind of problems a young twentysomething would obsess over: my career, my personal relationships, where I would be living in the future – or I'd be ruminating on the intricacies of Yemeni politics about which I was tasked with writing as a foreign reporter. The point is that I would be completely oblivious to the world around me. I could have been anywhere. But then a brief glance up from my phone as the taxi driver sped down 70th Street, and Sana'a would strike me. All at once, I would feel a rush of gratitude for being able to live amongst this beauty, among the good-naturedness of Yemenis, and Sana'a's bright sun. The stark desert mountains that surrounded the city, bathed in afternoon light, would force me to be present and grounded in the moment. They had a story to tell. May we all have the ears to listen.

Laura Kasinof, Washington DC, February 2025.

Notes

1. The Houthi rebels, also known as Ansar Allah, grew out of a religious revivalist group from the early 2000s associated with the Zaydi sect of Shia Islam, which perceived that northern Yemen was becoming overly influenced by Saudi-imported Wahhabi Islam. After Saleh's government killed the group's leader Badr al-Din al-Houthi in 2004, from whom the group takes its name, the Houthis became engaged in an on-again, off-again war with the Yemeni government for nearly a decade. When Saleh abdicated power in 2012, the group expanded its territorial control, starting in the far north of Yemen and working its way southward to Sana'a.

2. Geographically, on the map of Yemen, the two territories known as 'North' and 'South' might more accurately be seen as west and east, but these historical names have stuck.

3. Yemen has a centuries-long history of being ruled by an assortment of local sultans and imams, each presiding over overlapping pockets of territory. In 1839, the British empire set up a colonial outpost in Yemen's southern port city Aden, which in 1937, became the capital of a much expanded British colony of South Yemen. Meanwhile in northwestern Yemen, a dynasty of Zaydi Hashemite imams ruled, though an Ottoman occupying force controlled Sana'a and other northern cities to varying degrees from the mid 1800s until World War I. In 1962, the ruling imams and their loyalists in the North were overthrown by Republican revolutionaries, while in South Yemen, revolutionaries forced a British departure in 1967, establishing in their absence a Marxist state known as the People's Democratic Republic of Yemen. It was not until 1990 that these two Yemens merged to form the country that exists (albeit dividedly) today.

The Ruse of Sana'a

Rim Mugahed

Translated by Talei Lakeland

NOT A SOUL WILL believe what I am about to recount. But Sana'a, she knows – just as she knows I do not worry about revealing secret after secret, or making one mistake after another under her gaze. She will do nothing to me, just as she did nothing to the millions of others who perhaps did not carry secrets, who did not incite disorder – but who believed in Sana'a until she crushed them completely.

The sun is shining brightly despite the cold. A lady takes cover in the shade cast by the wall of the old gate. I imagine the cold she must be enduring for the sake of pale hands. The fortified wall sketches its shadow over the almost deserted square, and as the sun reflects off the white triangles crowning it, its shadow rests on the ground, where it is not yet ruptured by the hundreds of feet which will cross it. The gate, which has towered above for hundreds of years, keeps watch over the tales of those who enter and those who leave – never has it betrayed, yet neither has it been the most loyal. I look at it with love tinged with rancour. Once, I hid directly beneath it for fear of being hit by the shelling. I thought it impossible that a plane could consider shelling the gate – surely the gate would exist as long as Sana'a did. I was right – and yet, as I stood motionless against one of the gate's columns, the plane dropped a bomb not far away. I remained there, glued to the confined space under the gate's arch. Meanwhile, those who stood petrified up against the Old City's fortified walls, the gate and the other surrounding walls – once they realised where the target site was, and that the plane had left (perhaps seeking another target?) – stirred again and streamed away, screaming.

Did I move? Absolutely not – I remained motionless and, for a moment, forgot my caution. I began to sob in a forlorn, feminine voice, and my legs shook as I struggled to catch my breath. I wanted to squat down and bury my face in my arms as any young girl would have, but I was scared to be trampled beneath running feet, so I remained pressed up against the wall, no longer able to hold back my tears, which flowed profusely.

Why was I afraid? That is what I ask myself now. And why did I feel it was so important that I lived? My life had been devoid of meaning for years, but that pitiful, instinctive clinging still guided my days and nights, never ceasing to trap me in various existential rationalisations and justifications which wouldn't have convinced the great hole blown in the side of Faj Attan![1]

I have known only Sana'a, but Sana'a denies she knows me. She is older than my childhood in Hayel Street. The first scents to perfume my memory were the vegetables on 20th Street, the first sound to inhabit it the blare of the rubbish truck. My mother would scream frantically so that, from the ages of five to fifteen, I would hurry out carrying bags of rubbish she had prepared. When the beseeching sound of that vehicle fell silent, we all fell silent – we and the city. In its place, other sounds set up camp in our lives: the roar of warplanes, the death-whistle of rockets, the enormous explosions, the sound of gunshots being fired at various distances, the silence of ambulances after they stopped operating altogether, and finally the lamenting of the minarets that became a daily occurrence in every neighbourhood.

Today, I watch myself as I leave my street and head over towards busy Hayel Street. My head is turned by all the colourful clothes in the windows and the nonsensical names of the shops that are shut at this time of the morning when I'd normally be waiting for the bus to take me to the all-girls' school. My eyes scan the buses automatically: 'There must be schoolgirls inside, or at least four women! Never get on an empty bus, or a bus with only men on it' – as my mother would tell me, every day and night. Nor was I allowed to wait for school friends from the neighbourhood at their front doors, nor go up into the buildings they lived in under any circumstances, nor talk to their fathers or brothers. Nor was I allowed to eat or drink anything they offered me unless my girlfriends ate or drank it first. It seemed I was at risk of being kidnapped everywhere I went in Sana'a – on the bus, in neighbourhoods, in stairwells, at school, and in my girlfriends' homes. My mother had good reason to be terrified, just as there was good reason behind the fate she decided for me after what happened. Now, she tries to make me revert to the girl I was before, but she's too late, because even I can't find myself – no matter where I look.

I fidget in the sun, waiting for a crowd to gather so I can start working. I work as a 'lad' doing odd jobs in return for small amounts of money. Everybody here knows me, from Bab al-Yemen to Bab al-Salam[2] – the ladies call me to carry their shopping, shopkeepers send me to buy whatever they're running short of. Not once have I stolen, not once have I been late – and that's not all they like about me: they love that I keep my mouth shut. I break my silence only during arguments with my mother, or while singing to myself in a whisper once I'm alone. Keeping silent is in my interests, too: they used to pay me less than I deserved, but eventually they became embarrassed by my silence and failure to stick up for myself, so now they give me a fair price – and sometimes even more.

Many of them have tried to find out what my story is. They knew I could speak. And when they failed to get to the bottom of it, they made up stories themselves. I would hear some of the women speaking on my behalf: 'That poor boy lost his family in the bombing of Nuqum'[3]... 'The poor lad fled from al-Hudaydah'[4]... 'The boy is mute... the balatija[5] cut his tongue out'... I enjoyed hearing these stories, for none was any better or worse than what had actually happened to me.

As I touch my pocket to check I have enough money, an idea pops into my head. I jump up, walk towards the nearest café in the square, buy two khameer[6] and a cup of tea with milk, sit on the plastic chair and watch the buses pass by. I finish my meal quickly, then run towards where the buses congregate. My eyes quickly scan for the usual green sign on the front and back of the bus from Hayel to Bab al-Yemen. The bus is almost entirely full of women, while the two seats next to the driver are empty. I'm reminded of the old days when women's glances sought safety in mine, but then I remember I am no longer one of them. I get on and sit beside the driver, as I have done for the past six years. Silently, exhaustedly, onlookers chance upon my face for a moment, but then they leave me to my own company after seeing my thin, curveless body and my boyish, dull brown clothes.

The bus sets off, zigzagging through the old city and cutting through the crowds. The driver starts to race with other bus drivers, while I rely on my silence to recall the details.

Now we enter al-Zubairi Street, which appears untouched by the war. But how many others here have been touched by the war like me, I wonder. I scour the faces, buildings, billboards: there are so many of them... There I have my answer: pictures of those who died, young and old, are plastered on the walls and columns. The expressions on those boys' faces are sad, distracted. I imagine how they were killed, how their lives ended. But what was the use of plastering their pictures and names everywhere? Nothing but sorrow on the walls, nothing but questions: What futility is this? Why?

My mother had wanted to put up pictures of my father. She said we should write something dramatic under his image, like in the movies: 'He left, and hasn't been seen since'. But his colleague told her, 'He won't come back, even if you were to paint his picture on the sky itself!' My mother cried. Profusely. She inhaled the scent of his clothes and wallowed in yearning of pathological depths until she was no more than a shadow of the woman she had been. I was a teenager, torn between fear and casting everything into question. Each time I tried to recall what my father looked like, his face would disappear out of reach.

A few months after the war broke out, he had left for work as usual. He worked for a government authority – I don't know what his job title was. We were very average people – distinguished neither by heroism nor misfortune – colourless, voiceless. My father left for work in the morning, I went to school, and my younger brothers went to their schools as well, while my mother drowned in housework and in the worry that something would happen to one of them. We waited for my father all afternoon. My mother called him several times. There had been no shelling that day, so it was unlikely he had been killed in an aerial bombardment. We waited until night-time. We waited until the next evening. We carried on waiting, and as we waited, our lives came to a standstill.

My mother went to his place of work and introduced herself to one of the men working there. He told her to keep her mouth shut and not to speak to anyone else. He quickly sent for another man, who approached her and introduced himself. She realised she knew him – he was a friend of my father's who would come to him all the time. He whispered in her ear that 'they' had come and taken him. She didn't know who 'they' were, so she asked him, confused. In an even quieter whisper, he replied, '*the Houthis!*' Then he gave her the advice my mother regrets taking every day: 'Do not go looking for him – or you and your daughter could run into some problems. I will try and transfer his monthly salary and bring it to you at the end of each month.' My mother believed him. She came home and wailed with all her might, slapped her chest and tore her hair out. Her pain was devastating to witness. Never had I imagined that pain of such magnitude could exist. My mother forbade us to tell anyone. We were to say my father was travelling. But the truth was my father wasn't coming back.

That marked the beginning of many long nights, during which my mother would check time after time that the door was locked, talk to herself out loud, make up lies and stories to her family. She refused outright to accept what had happened, and clung onto the hope that my father would return, as he was neither a politician, nor a journalist, nor an opposition member of any kind. As I said, he was the epitome of the average citizen.

To our misfortune, the state stopped paying civil servants' salaries. My father's colleague informed my mother of this. Disaster, once again, was knocking on our door. This time, my mother's panic reached a whole new level – she became completely crazy and devoid of reason. With hindsight, it seems only logical that neither the war, nor the spectre of death that hung over us day and night, nor the huge crack in the wall of our house caused by the Faj Attan bombing[7] (along with the prospect of the house caving in on us and the neighbours)... none of these terrified my mother as much as the realisation that we had no income. With this in mind, she told us we were going to travel to see her relatives and live with them. I can almost laugh now, but my mother was directly in fate's firing line. Fate had put her there and had perhaps conspired with a reckless friend to say, 'Let us see exactly how much this woman can withstand!'

I was sad to be leaving Sana'a, the kind of sadness I wouldn't have dared admit to in front of my mother. I remember how, in a moment of premature nostalgia, I went out into the street to fetch something for my mother, and lingered there to muse for a moment: on the one lone tree, on the balconies covered so that women could hang out their washing without being seen; on the bolted iron gates; on the street corner where teenagers hung out, snacking on pumpkin and sunflower seeds whose shells had accumulated in the gutter for years. I lingered on the house we lived in. I knew nothing else but this neighbourhood – it was here that I played, ran, grew up; here that I wove together dreams which would never come true. Sorrow overcame me, so I returned home. I remember my mother's face when I came through the door. She was in total shock – as though she had seen a vision, or dancing swans, or some criminal being awarded a prize. Her expression said, 'Never! I don't believe it! Impossible!'

As for me, I stopped at the door, taken aback by her expression. My melancholy and nostalgia evaporated in an instant, only to be replaced by terror as my mother began to laugh – a hysterical laugh which no fifteen-year-old could possibly comprehend.

Now I understand...

My mother, who had started preparing to leave Sana'a, was wondering how to tell her family everything. She called her brother in advance, but he told her their neighbourhood had been bombed by the Houthis. They had fled two nights earlier with nothing but the clothes on their backs, and were now staying in a refugee camp.

It was my uncle who needed my mother's help...

I do not know what was said in that phone call, but it brought about the end of my life as I'd known it. A few months later, I was no longer the slender girl with small eyes and a high-pitched voice who went to the all-girls' school on Hayel Street – I had become a boy with smooth hair and a face with no identity, wearing strange clothes and searching for work, returning home each night to an unremarkable, untidy neighbourhood in Sana'a's al-Thawra quarter. Terror gripped me for years. Every night as I was walking home carrying bread, I completely forgot that I was a boy. Even if I had remembered, my mother had told me they don't spare anyone here: they rape girls, boys, and animals, and after raping them they rip out their insides and throw them in the rubbish.

I didn't blame her. My brothers were twelve and ten, so what could they possibly have done to provide for us? We had to live, so my mother decided that even though I hadn't worked before, in a neighbourhood like this one I would have to be a boy, and we had to stay in a neighbourhood like this one because it was the cheapest place to live in Sana'a. She coached me in how to talk and stand and behave, she taught me the basics of being male, and she thanked God sincerely that I was neither beautiful nor shapely, that I was endowed with neither a bosom nor buttocks. She thanked God for my strange voice, my strange face and my strange nature – everything she had worried about previously she became grateful for.

I did all kinds of jobs. I begged. All that mattered was to come home with bread in the evening – plenty of bread which would last us the next day – and to bring home some money, even if just a little, for water. Anything else was a luxury. My mother cooked once a week after having saved up to buy a quarter of a chicken or something like that.

My mother was truly grateful for me...

I lost my voice, I no longer spoke, and there were nights when I tried out my newfound masculinity – I slept in the open air, driving my mother crazy. Lately, though, she has started to get used to it.

The bus cascades down from al-Zubairi Bridge. Back in the day, pictures of Nancy Ajram[8] had covered the pillars of this bridge, and the banks on both sides stood proud with images of elegant young men and women, the likes of whom we wanted to grow up to emulate. On top of the Ministry of Youth and Sport there had been a huge sign with a picture of a beautiful, smiling young woman. Now, all the pictures were of those killed in the war, or signs urging people to martyr themselves in holy war.

As the bus turns a corner I smile to myself. Here's Hayel, there's the Panorama Hotel, those are Hayel's residential buildings, and this is the petrol station where cars wait in endless queues. I signal to the driver that I am mute, but he carries on talking to me anyway. I don't listen to him until he says something strange.

'I may talk a lot, but I wish I were mute like you.'

I look at him, surprised, so he answers, 'Son, you have no idea how many men have died because they couldn't hold their tongues... They kill them for the sake of a word. What's the use of being able to speak in this day and age?'

He has a point, and I believe him. I remember my father. He had said something – he must have said something.

The bus crawls along. The crowds in the street are very animated, and even though I have been away for years, it looks the same: all those sellers, the countless women's clothes shops, the mannequins wearing elegant, colourful outfits, and women with an insatiable appetite for shopping.

Do I miss being female?

I don't know – I've never had time to think about that.

Near the roundabout on 20th Street, I signal to the driver to stop. He does as I say, takes the fare, and as he thanks me, his glance lingers on my face. That always happens to me, but I make no expression to betray my guilt or fear – I remain frozen as though I haven't noticed anything.

I turn towards 20th Street, which is still as filthy as it always was: a sprawling neighbourhood. I hurry towards the fruit and vegetable sellers, trying to locate that scent which was my first memory of smell. The street is just as it used to be, and the sellers too, even though there are fewer of them. I walk among them, and of course none would remember me. In a way, that's reassuring. I leave them and head towards where we used to live, strolling through noisy alleyways before I get there, crossing over next to the mosque. Our flat was in a building near the mosque.

When I get to the four-storey building, I stop. How is it possible for us not to stay on the path we've chosen for ourselves? Which power has the right to sketch out unwanted fates, fates that we refuse to accept even if they're realities we've been forced to live out? Here is the balcony, there are the windows. Between those walls, my mother's incense once filled the air. What smell fills the home now, I wonder?

I sit down on the pavement opposite and stop looking up. I spent my whole childhood playing in this neighbourhood. At twelve I dressed up in a hijab and play-acted being a grown woman. I dreamt of marrying the boy next door and living a little further away for a while so my mother would miss me, come and visit me. I accompanied my mother to all the wedding parties in the neighbourhood, and always knew who was in love with whom and if they were going to get married or not.

How strange it is when your life is no more than history...

My mother left no trace of us – she told no one where she was going. She even cut off all contact with my father's family, who lived in another city; she cut off almost everyone we knew. Nobody knew us anymore, and it became impossible to get hold of us. We disappeared, just as my father had. She told me it would be temporary, so that nobody would find me out, and as soon as my brothers had grown up, I would return to how I was, and she would get back in touch with people. But even when my brothers came of age, I still refused to go back to what I had been. I had nothing left to return to, so I decided to remain as I was. My mother cried, begged, threatened, incited my brothers to turn against me, but I no longer cried out to anything or anyone, and nobody could stop me: I had become male!

I leave the neighbourhood and walk downhill towards the ring road. I'm no longer thinking of anything – my consciousness has become a blank slate. I just walk in whichever direction I want, and when I cross over beside Hayel Park, I decide to enter. One of the spontaneous decisions I make today. I am angry at myself, angry at my self-pity, angry I expected a life other than this one, so I allow this anger to take up space in my whole abdomen.

The park still has a children's play area, and there are a few children playing with their mothers, as well as boys by themselves, girls too, and grown-up men with no reason to be there. I walk here and there – I don't want to draw attention to myself. I decide to leave through the other gate, next to which I notice a man with a thick beard. He seems as empty as I am. I walk towards him, and before passing him towards the exit, I stop despite myself, contemplating his features. And just as obscurity is unexpectedly illuminated, as the first word of love your mother utters passes right through you, as fireflies light up a dark passageway, and as history can be upended to reveal no more than a ruse, I find myself approaching the man and saying, in disbelief, '*Abi!* My father!'

The man looks at me in astonishment, as though we are sharing our recognition of a ruse Sana'a crafted with her own hands. I utter his name, his father's name, and his grandfather's name.[9] He stands up as though the names have pierced right through him. I do not wait for him to nod. As I laugh, all I can see is my mother rising again like the sun, her hands adorned with henna!

Notes

1. A mountain targeted by a strike on a missile base in Sana'a in April 2015 as part of the Saudi-led bombing campaign.
2. Bab al-Yemen and Bab al-Sabah are two of the nine gates that serve as the only access points to the old city. Others include Bab al-Shagadeef, and Bab Sha'ub.
3. Mountain in Sana'a which was subjected to heavy bombardment in 2015 by the Saudi-led alliance. The mountain contained an arms depot, and as the depot exploded, rockets were launched over Sana'a. The total number of victims remains unknown.
4. Yemeni city on the Red Sea coast.
5. Pro-government thugs accused of assisting the crackdown on protesters during the rule of former President Ali Abdullah Saleh.
6. Yemeni bread fried in oil.
7. A neighbourhood of Sana'a which, on 25 August 2017, was bombed by the government's Saudi-led military coalition, killing at least fourteen civilians, six of them children. The Saudi military leaders later admitted it was a 'technical mistake'.
8. Lebanese singer famous throughout the Arab world.
9. In the Arabic tradition, people adopt their father's name, and their grandfather's name as their middle names.

Borrowing a Head

Abdoo Taj

Translated by Andrew Leber

WHEN MY HEAD FELL off, there on the street, I wasn't going to bother picking it up. But people were shouting – 'Your head! Your head!' – so I told myself maybe it wasn't appropriate to leave my head in front of them like that. My hands felt around until I gently picked it up.

I set it back down on my neck – longest in the family! – and went on walking briskly towards the junction. There, the bus would take me right to where I had promised Reyhana I would meet her.

'Baaaab al-Yemen?' I yelled at the bus driver. He nodded in agreement, so I stepped aboard.

The bus was playing the song 'Alam Siri'[1] as it crept along. The driver moved slowly out of fear of hitting one of the many potholes on Sha'ub Street – the bus would bang around, and heads would fall. Still, the driver got carried away with the rhythm of the song. As it sped up – *Alam Siri, Alam Siri... Ala Bismillah Al-Rahman* – he sped up too, until one of the passengers shouted out, 'There are women on this bus!'

Of course, the driver immediately slowed down. It would be deeply shameful for a woman's head to fall off. (Even though every time I've seen a women's head fall off, it stayed

13

covered up – nothing to be seen.) Much as I didn't care about any of this – really, not at all! – I still yell for the bus to slow down whenever I happen to be in a bus with women on it, as I personally feel uncomfortable when the bus rattles its way over an especially large pothole.

The bus suddenly stopped right next to an old man and his wife. The grey-haired man sat down next to me, while the old lady headed towards the other women. *What if I swapped heads with this old fellow?* I wondered. I felt a deep thirst to peek into this life I knew nothing about, the curiosity almost overpowering. *He looks to be at least 70 – his life must be interesting!* My appetite for borrowing heads knows no limits.

A month ago, I agreed (under duress) to lend my head to my cousin, Bashir. He had returned from Shar'ab[2] without a head, and one evening he clenched his hands into fists, beseeching me for my head. I flatly refused. I hate spending gloomy evenings without thinking or chatting, just like I hate sleeping the days away. (Still, I recently gave up my bad habit of sleeping with my body on the bed and my head on the windowsill, Bluetooth headphones in place.) But having said all this, I did feel sorry for Bashir – nothing more boring than spending all day long in his condition!

Ever since he started borrowing my head, our memories have started to mix. Yesterday he went to the mosque to pray the maghrib prayer.[3] My head knows it was difficult for him, but he still forced himself to go through with it. Even now, I hear the imam in my head, reciting 'Surah Ad-Duhaa' during the first *raka'ah*.[4] Of course, my cousin struggled to follow along, just as you would if your limbs all felt at odds with your mind.

He also went to the grocery store, bought some of those cheap cigarettes, and sat smoking and relaxing while he watched passersby. There are no secrets between us anymore, as sometimes his body retains some exciting memory that he unwittingly empties into my head.

14

What draws me to start pilfering his memories is one particularly warm recollection – details from an Eid celebration, it seems. Up on a grey cement roof, among family, with plenty of stewed and slow-cooked meat, steaming hot, in clay pots. Lots of women bring dishes to the gathering. The smell of fireworks in the air. Children wearing new clothes, the fabric giving off that unique scent that always captivates me when I inhale it. The smell of meat roasting on the coals inside its tinfoil. A mother's hand wreathed in henna picking up empty pots from the spread. All intimate moments that I look at as if through my own eyes, a memory of when he felt he could never be happier.

I couldn't resist my fascination with this memory, and one day I decided to ask him where it came from. He'd never lived a day in a village like the one in this memory! Could he have gained it from somebody else...? But to answer any of my questions, we'd need a spare head for him.

I snapped out of my daydream as I noticed the driver turn right. As the bus plodded along, I read the sign for 'Al-Biruni Clinic' – the only one I recognised on a road filled with hard-to-memorise shop names. The bus kept moving, heedless of the thoughts boiling over in my head. Every so often passengers called out stops, until the bus finally escaped the afternoon traffic, arrived at Bab al-Yemen, and I got off.

My head fell off for the second time. It rolled along down the road, like an empty can blown by the wind, as I kept running after it. A passerby finally stopped it and gave it back to me. (I meant to say 'thank you' but didn't finish putting the head back on in time.)

I fixed it back in place. Taking out a comb and mirror from my bag, I combed the hair smooth, dusted it off, and said to it, 'There's a good noggin,' patting it as if it were my dog. I walked along the pavement until I turned right, heading towards Old Sana'a to wait for Reyhana, where she would arrive in a quarter of an hour.

The weather was hot as hell. I took shelter under a leafy tree, sitting and watching people walk by: gloomy faces; a dog's rotting corpse that people trampled on carelessly; a person who put his head on a chair as though he were setting down a jacket, before leaving it to go buy ice cream. Not everyone is curious about what happens to heads. One thing I've learned since the war broke out is that people try to steer clear of their heads as though they were landmines. They flee painful memories that their heads tempt them to revisit.

Reyhana arrived, wearing her beautiful hat. We went wandering around Sana'a, intoxicated by the opportunity to be together after so much longing. 'The weather's too hot,' I said to her. 'Let's follow the alleyways and stay in the shade.' She was sweating too, so she agreed.

We walked and talked. Our eyes betrayed a wish that we could get away from all these other people – maybe duck behind a banana seller's cart, or into a jewellery shop. Just leave everybody behind and kiss each other as we listened to songs. I imagined all of this as her scent wafted over me. I like the way Reyhana smells.

We went to the Burj al-Salam Hotel, an attraction for tourists who have no connection to Sana'a. At the top, though, there is a magical view of the old city as well as the new.

'Hello! I'd like to go to the top of the building,' I said as I entered.

'Do you have ID?' the reception responded. 'Proof of marriage?'

'No,' I lied, 'she's my sister!'

Reyhana could have been my sister, with her wide eyes and wheat-gold complexion. But he would only be convinced by ID. We tried to negotiate with him but after a while he dismissed us rudely.

I felt bad. We made our way slowly back to Bab al-Yemen amid eyes that viewed us with suspicion, or tried to get us to buy things – children's clothes, fake silver rings, things I'd never even thought of buying because they were so trivial. I suggested we go to the raisin-juice seller – it always tasted so good. But he said they had run out. 'Do you want barley water instead?' he suggested. To me, barley was also trivial. We headed back to the centre of the old town, right where we had started.

We meandered among the alleys. As Reyhana looked up at an exquisite Sana'a house, she seemed puzzled. 'You know what's so beautiful about old Sana'a? These are just ordinary houses.' I told her that the architectural design was very old, and that the original design must have formed in someone's head centuries ago and yet it survives to this day. Centuries seemed to me like eternity, something that called out for wonder and amazement. Yet she was not amazed.

Even though I'd eaten before I set out, I began to feel hungry. My energy levels sank (you know, that uncomfortable feeling that you're about to collapse). *I don't get it*, I thought. *Maybe I didn't eat lunch?* But no, I had eaten. There was no reason for this. A person can go eight weeks without eating, I read recently, which is two months. It should take time for my energy to run low, or my blood sugar to drop, or for me to die (for example); nevertheless, I was starting to fade.

I told Reyhana, suggesting we take a break and get a sandwich. She preferred that I go pick them up, so I did. We were sitting under a tree eating them, when she asked me suddenly about happiness.

'I don't think I have a right to talk about happiness,' I replied, 'because I have never tasted it.'

Reyhana doesn't know what I hide from everyone – that I feel extremely anxious whenever I'm in a space where I don't feel comfortable. I feel like my heart is pounding and that I'm going to faint. *Where does this come from?* I've wondered many times.

Was it just irritable bowels, that I suffer from a lot, or an unknown mental illness? I had searched the internet but it didn't help me. The condition struck me now while I was still sitting there with Reyhana, absent-minded. I felt the fear bubble up inside me, like a gentle stream. I felt a faint pounding in my ears. I got up, telling Reyhana that I was feeling anxious and couldn't remain seated. But she thought that I was trying to avoid talking to her, and she didn't believe me. What else for me to do but take off my head for her to make sure.

Notes

1. A popular Yemeni song (the title translates as 'If You Don't Mind' by Mohamed Morshed Naji, based on a poem by the Yemeni poet Ahmed el-Jabri (1937-2024), in turn inspired by 'Ala Imsiri', a traditional song to accompany the bride on her way from her parents' house to the groom's house on the day of the wedding.
2. Shar'ab is a region near the city of Taiz in western Yemen, about a 175 miles south of Sana'a.
3. Prayer at sunset.
4. One of a number of supplications performed during Muslim prayer.

The Jacket

Wajdan Al-Shathali

Translated by Majd Abu Shawish

To my friend, Omar Bin Abdelaziz Bin Akil

WE GOT TIRED OF lazy chatting, arguing and laughing about political, cultural and critical topics.

We got tired of comments, precise and passing remarks, serious and mocking notes about the road, the passengers and the inhabitants of the city where the bus had stopped for a break.

Each one of us had sunk in his seat, entered into his own world, and begun to feel the silence of his thoughts as the road went by.

Ahmed, Omar and I were the three lucky ones chosen to take this trip so as to represent the Hadramout Governorate in a creative writing workshop organised by the Cultural Centre of Sana'a. Or perhaps we were the unlucky ones, Omar suggested, because such workshops and cultural activities were never held in Hadramout.

'On the way to Sana'a, there was everything but Sana'a.'

We had to pass through three authorities, 30 checkpoints and endure 27 hours of physical and mental discomfort, before

Sana'a finally smiled at us and said, 'Welcome!'

Immediately after getting off the bus, as we were still trying to collect ourselves following this marathon journey, Omar's voice broke our silence and exhaustion: 'Do you know why the oxygen level in Sana'a is lower than anywhere else?'

We were used to such questions, which Omar would ask for some reason or no reason all day long. However you answered them, your answer would be wrong because Omar always had his own answer ready for each question he asked.

Despite knowing all this, I decided to answer him using logic and science, as most other people would. But Ahmed beat me to it, saying: 'Because Sana'a is so high above sea level.'

As expected, Omar answered: 'A classic and woeful misconception! Can't you see what I see?!' He nodded his head towards two beautiful women on the opposite pavement, trying to cross the road towards us. 'Look! Aren't the beauties walking in the streets of Sana'a capable of sucking the oxygen out of an entire galaxy?'

The three of us laughed.

I suggested we all stay in a hotel in al-Jadeeda neighbourhood that I stay in every time I visit Sana'a. I didn't know, then, whether I was merely suggesting the place, or outright ordering them where to go. Either way, they had no grounds to object; this was their first visit and they knew very well how familiar I was with the city, having more than four years' experience of finding my way around its streets.

At the hotel, after we unpacked, I suggested that we go out for dinner and explore a little. Ahmed said he was tired, adding: 'Why don't you go out and get us some food? We have a long day ahead of us tomorrow, so we should have an early night.' Omar concurred and I had no choice but to agree.

Going down the stairs, I thought of a good restaurant two blocks away that I could easily walk to. I crossed the main road and took a shortcut down a side street. Suddenly, I found myself in front of military barracks. Everything then became incomprehensible.

Two gunshots made me freeze to the spot. Then I heard a voice ordering me to take my jacket off and another telling me to put my hands above my head.

In such times and circumstances, no one knows how it is that every organ of one's body develops its own ear, its own mind, its own soul!

As I received the soldiers' orders and warnings – 'Take your jacket off slowly. Place it on the ground. Hands above your head. On your knees. Lie face down.' – I could tell that the body parts these instructions were intended for carried them out instantly, before my ears picked them up, certainly before my brain processed them. I saw how every individual body part was desperate to survive.

There were four of them, heavily armed soldiers carrying automatic weapons. One of them came over to me as I lay face-down. He checked my jacket lying next to me with the muzzle of his gun. Then, he asked me to show him my ID. I struggled to find my voice.

Another soldier – I have no idea how he ended up behind me – found it necessary to poke me on the lower back with the butt of his riffle. With a groan of pain I re-found my words. I told them that my ID card was in the pocket of my jacket, and I explained everything about the journey, from getting on the bus in Hadramout to reaching the hotel and going out to get food and the bad luck that led me down this side street.

They decided to let me go, warning me not to take this street again; as if I was going to come here ever again after what had happened!

I took my Jacket and ID card back and fled the street. I quickened my pace until I reached the street I was originally aiming for. On my way, I walked past many restaurants that had closed. At last, at the end of the street, there was a restaurant with its lights on.

Through the glass window, I saw two men standing in front of the cashier, with their backs towards me. At the far end of the restaurant's hall, also with his back to me, was a broad-shouldered man sitting at a corner table. The way his body was moving, it was obvious that he was chewing his food voraciously. This was sufficient evidence that the restaurant was still open and serving food.

I pushed the door and entered. But as soon as I set foot in the place, the previous scene was repeated. The two men in front of the cashier turned, pointed their guns in my face, and started shouting. 'Take your jacket off slowly and drop it to the floor! Two steps backward! Stand straight. Put your hands above your head!'

I tried to stand straight but my feet wouldn't respond. They approached me. One of them started to frisk me carefully and the other, even more carefully, went through my jacket.

I explained to them what had happened just five minutes earlier. They laughed. One of them pointed at the cashier and asked him to take my order. I took my food and left, taking a different route back, knowing it would add another block to my journey, but telling myself it was worth it.

As soon as I turned off the street the restaurant was on, I found myself in front of yet another military barracks. 'Stop! Take off your jacket! Hands up! Lay down on the floor!' I dropped the food, took my jacket off and got down on the ground next to it.

I heard a gunshot. Then I saw one of the soldiers fall and start writhing and screaming from the pain. Blood was spouting from the base of his neck.

The sound of bullets echoed in all directions. Glass from the windows of houses fell and scattered across the tarmac. Women and children started to scream behind those windows.

I stayed on the ground with my face pressed to the tarmac. After a short while, I saw one of the soldiers crawling towards one of the narrow alleys. I followed him, copying his movements, leaving everything else behind. I crawled and crawled until I reached the end of that alley. Then I stood up and ran as fast as I could until I reached the hotel.

As soon as I finished telling Ahmed and Omar the story of what had happened, they started laughing hysterically. While Ahmed was rolling on the floor convulsing with laughter, Omar was struggling to say something, but also trying to stop laughing. He could only say a couple of words between each intake of breath:

'But you...' then a burst of laughter,

'Your jacket...' then a gasp of laughter,

'You forgot...' then more gasping.

When he found himself unable to finish his sentence, he pointed his finger at the back of the door. I followed the direction of his finger and saw my jacket hanging behind the door, exactly where I left it when we first arrived at the hotel.

The General Secretariat of Speed Bumps

Hayel Al Mathabi

Translated by Christiaan James

IT IS AN INDISPUTABLE fact that the mayor of the capital, Mr. Amin Sa'dan, was one of very few men recognised for his unyielding integrity and exacting moral rectitude, for it was he who absolutely refused to appoint his wife's brother, Sami Sarhan, as a bureaucrat within the Capital Municipality till all legally mandated measures had been carried out. And so, summoning forth the director general for administrative affairs of the municipality, Mr. Amin conveyed to him his desire to find a suitable position for his brother-in-law.

Proud as could be, the director general for administrative affairs circled back to Mayor Sa'dan, informing him that he had indeed identified a vacant position for Sami: engineering director for the Office of Roadways at the municipality. Mayor Sa'dan noted: 'While it is accurate to say that Sami does not hold a bachelor's degree in engineering per se, he does however have a B.A. in literature from the Department of History,' to which the director general confirmed that this very engineering position specifically called for an undergraduate degree in literature from a history department.

And so, just days later, a job advert from the capital municipality appeared in the newspapers:

The Capital Municipality of Sana'a hereby announces a vacancy for Director of Engineering within the Office of Roadways subject to the following conditions:

Applicants for this engineering position must hold a bachelor's degree in literature from the University of Sana'a, Faculty of Literature (Department of History), Cohort 35, Class of 2003. Any applicant holding an engineering degree is hereby excluded and will not be considered;

At the time of the personal interview, the applicant must be 24 years, 3 months, and 11 days old;

The applicant must wear glasses and have a neck mole directly below the left ear;

The applicant must have undergone a tonsillectomy on January 4, 1996 at Al-Thawra Hospital in Sana'a;

Height must measure exactly 174 centimetres;

Applicant shall reside on Hadda Street and his municipality-issued ID card must be 5532;

His name must be Sami Sarhan, and;

He must have a brother two years his junior named Hani Sarhan.

These conditions having been met, a personal interview will be arranged for applicants on the 17th September. The top candidate will enter in as a Schedule 5 appointee with the following employment-based compensatory allowances: 10,000 riyals for streets; 15,000 riyals for pavements; 10,000 riyals transportation allowance; 10,000 riyals for non-transportation allowances; and 20,000 riyals for finding oneself on streets far removed from his residence.

The ever-so-scrupulous Amin Sa'dan expressed his utter

astonishment to the director general for administrative affairs when no one put forth their application for the position save one person: Sami Sarhan. Mr. Amin underscored and stressed that to ensure equal opportunity for all (as stipulated by law) he had widely circulated the advert in the papers. So why then had applicants refrained from applying?!

The director general for administrative affairs was even more perplexed than he was. His lips pursed, he said to the capital mayor: 'Wallahi,[1] I have no clue, Ustaaz Amin![2]'

And so Sami sat before the interview committee which had codified a fair and objective system whereby each question would be allocated ten marks. The committee's first question for Sami was whether he had at times walked along Mohammed Mahmoud Al-Zubairi Street. Answering affirmatively, a committee member probed further:

'After which of the revolutionaries was Zubairi Street named?'

Sami responded, 'Leader Al-Sallal.'[3]

Letting out a knowing laugh, another panellist explained to the rest of the members what Sami Sarhan had intended to say. Simply put, Zubairi Street had initially been named after Leader Al-Sallal and that, although the street was now named after Zubairi, Sami meant that it had originally been named in honour of Al-Sallal.

Questions from the interview committee continued to flow, one right after the other:

'How are you, Mr. Sami?'

To which he responded: 'May God protect you.'

Here the committee marked down another ten points for the correct answer.

'What is your full tripartite name, Mr. Sami?'

'Sami Khalil Sarhan.'

The committee notated an additional ten marks.

'What time is it, Mr. Sami?'

'It's a quarter to 11.'

Ten more points for an accurate response.

'What's your address, Mr. Sami?'

'Hayy Al-Medina, Hadda Street.'

Ten marks for yet another spot-on answer.

So Sami became director of engineering in the Office of Roadways Administration at the Capital Municipality of Sana'a. And though he held just a bachelor's degree from a history department, his official title was elevated to Engineer Sami Sarhan, after which official correspondence began to arrive at the municipality addressed to Mr Historical Engineer Sami Sarhan, Director of Engineering.

And so events progressed and everything would have passed smoothly had it not been for that idiot Naji Hassan, currently serving as undersecretary for the Legal Affairs Department. Naji Hassan was an engineer and had received engineering degrees from universities in Sana'a and Germany, advancing within the municipality till finally becoming head of the Department of Engineering in the Office of Roadways. When the mayor first had approached the director general for administrative affairs about finding a job for Sami, the very next day the director made a surprising observation, something he had not noticed before: Engineer Naji Hassan was incompetent at his job, as head of engineering, and was summarily transferred to serve as head of the legal department, where he could show his chops as a bureaucrat in legal affairs. However, he failed miserably at writing briefs. A compassionate man, Mayor Sa'dan advised giving Naji Hassan a third chance to prove his salt and thus got him transferred to take charge of the medical department. However, it was absolutely lamentable that here, a man, on whom the state had expended so much to pursue studies at the largest university in Germany, had not a clue how to use a stethoscope to examine patients, nor did he have the slightest idea how to operate a blood pressure machine or even – in the absence of an attending nurse –

administer a jab to a patient at an external clinic. All that, despite the fact that the municipality had in no way skimped on or short-changed him in the least, having put at his disposal a vehicle adorned with Red Crescent licence plates in order to examine municipality patients at their homes, and even provided him with an operating theatre equipped with the latest in surgical gadgetry. Yet, despite it all, he refused to perform an appendectomy on a functionary in a critical condition whose appendix was about to burst. Out of laziness and inaction, he transferred the worker to the general hospital where he died.

Based on such incompetency and malpractice, the mayor could have shown Engineer Naji Hassan the door, but the gentleman was truly merciful and saw it only right to offer him a fourth chance, reinstating him as undersecretary of legal affairs. The head of the legal department was consequently shuffled over to the Department of Electrical Units whereafter Mahmoud Saleh, the accountant, took up the reins at Medical. Undoubtedly, through such directives, Mayor Sa'dan offered excellent opportunities to those underperforming at one post to shine in another where their talents might be better suited.

Some felt that Engineer Naji Hassan was an obnoxious, ungrateful man, entirely unappreciative of the mayor's humane touch, and he openly cursed Amin Sa'dan all over town. However, the director general for administrative affairs discovered that it was not a matter of ingratitude or boorishness, but rather a mental defect. The director general revealed to Amin Sa'dan that he had walked in on Engineer Naji Hassan only to discover him talking to himself, raving madly in strange, incomprehensible gibberish. Immediately, Amin Sa'dan summoned Mahmoud Saleh, the sometime accountant now head of the medical department. He ordered him to place Engineer Naji Hassan, head of legal affairs, under medical observation and to urgently draft a medical report on the state of his mental health. Amin Sa'dan assured Mahmoud the accountant that a successful undertaking of this assignment would confirm his impeccable medical competencies and just might qualify him to assume the role of DG for administrative affairs that would soon be vacated following the appointment of the current director as director general of the capital municipality itself.

Mahmoud Saleh the accountant left Amin Sa'dan's office gung ho to prove his fitness as the Medical Department director. Several days later, he returned with his clinical assessment of Engineer Naji Hassan's mental state. He sat across from Amin Sa'dan, who held the report and skimmed what the accountant had drafted:

> Mental Balance of Engineer Naji Hassan:
> If we look at the capital as well as fixed and movable assets in the brain of Engineer Naji Hassan, and closely analyse the consumption rate of said capital, that being his head....

At which point, Mr Amin Sa'dan indignantly hurled the financial report of Engineer Naji Hassan's mind and reamed into Mahmoud the accountant for his medical ignorance. Everything crescendoed till finally Mahmoud Saleh, the erstwhile accountant, was transferred over as technical advisor for the Department of Electrical Operations and the director of Mechanical Units took charge of Medical.

To take the wind out of loony Naji Hassan's claim that Mayor Sa'dan had purloined his original position to give to his wife's brother, it was decided a new General Administration for Speed Bumps should be set up, to be overseen (with rank of director general) by Historical Engineer Sami Sarhan.

Sent abroad on a delegation at the expense of the municipality, Historical Engineer Sami Sarhan returned a fully-fledged expert in the science of 'Speedbumpology', which he had studied while overseas. Sami Sarhan became something of a passing scientific sensation, for his historical studies had played no small part in the development of Speedbumpology. With just one glance at any speed bump on any street in Sana'a, he could determine the bump's age, the reason for it, and its history. Given the import of speed bumps in the lives of Yemenis today, Mayor Sa'dan established an institute annexed to the General Administration for Speed Bumps – The Higher Institute for Speed Bumps – wherein the institute's dean, Historical Engineer Sami Sarhan himself, began delivering lectures to department employees and students alike who had enrolled in a course of studies.

With keen foresight, Mayor Amin Sa'dan decided to take pre-emptive steps to thwart any attempt to later pilfer speed bumps now that they had become a national and archaeological treasure, particularly so after the establishment of a specialised institute. And so to keep speed bumps under the exclusive purview of the Capital Municipality of Sana'a, Amin Sa'dan changed the municipality's name to the General Secretariat for Speed Bumps!

Notes

1. 'I swear.'
2. 'Mister.'
3. Abdallah al-Sallal (1917-1994) was the first President of the Yemen Arab Republic (North Yemen) from September 1962 until his removal in November 1967. Previously, he had been the leader of the North Yemeni Revolution of 1962.

The Road to Destiny

Atiaf Alwazir

Translated by Maisa Almanasreh

LITTLE DID RAJA' KNOW, that the day she begged our parents to go to Hakku al-Khair farm would be her last.

On Wednesday afternoon, the 1st of Shawwal,1386,[1] Raja' and I were playing a tongue twister out in the courtyard, just off the alleyways of Al-Abhar neighbourhood, named after the largest artery in the human body. We challenged each other to say this sentence as quickly as possible without making any mistakes:

'A white chicken laid an egg on the rooftop of a white mosque. Why did you, white chicken, lay an egg on the rooftop of a white mosque?'

I won the game, but Raja' wouldn't accept defeat. So, she took out some marbles from her pocket and said: 'Let's play Zurgaif, but on one condition: if I win, help me convince our parents to go to Hakku al-Khair; and if you win, I'll accept that we'll stay here.'

I agreed to this condition, trusting God's will. And yet, somehow, I believed we still had some power to determine the future.

We dug a small hole in the ground. Then we began the game. My sister started. She threw two marbles into the sky simultaneously, and we watched them fall to the ground. One of them fell into the designated hole and the other one landed outside it, which was the goal of the game. She jumped up and down and danced around me in celebration.

Suddenly, we heard someone clapping from the top floor of the building. We guessed right away that it was Umi.[2] Looking up at the window, we could see her standing there all covered up, with only her smoky, kohl-lined eyes clearly visible. She clapped again.

We pointed to the jackets we wore, reassuring our mother that we were protected despite the unusually cold winter.

I presumed from the way she then closed the window, and didn't open it again, that Umi was satisfied. So, we restarted our game: it was my turn now. I flicked two marbles into the sky, and we watched them land on the ground and roll until they both fell into the designated hole. My sister screamed: 'Kish Kish', meaning get out of here, you lost.

Since I lost, I had no choice but to accept that we might go to Hakku al-Khair in Bani Hushaish village. The farm house was initially named 'Hakku al-Kalb', meaning the 'estate of the dog' because the villagers had found a statue there that looked like a dog. But when my grandfather bought it, he didn't like that name, so he changed it to 'Hakku al-Khair', which meant the 'estate of goodness.'

I loved the farm, but I wanted to understand why my sister was so obsessed with going there on that specific day.

'What's waiting for you over there? Why do we need to go today?' I asked.

'Are you serious? Why in the world would we stay here? All we do is sit around all day, clean the house, and wash the qat. There's no school or fresh air. At least over there we can play with the goats and eat grapes.'

'I swear, you're the biggest goat. It's not even grape season right now, you idiot. It's cold outside.'

'So what, even if it's not grape season, it's raisins season.

Now who's the idiot, ha? Me or you?'

My sister was not wrong: staying in Sana'a was pointless. The schools were closed because of the fighting, and going to the farm would be an opportunity to play in a clean, healthy, and peaceful environment. It would take us away from this war that started five years ago between the Republicans and the Royalists,[3] with each side always claiming they're about to succeed, and that the war is about to stop.

This war took away our school, despite both sides claiming that they care about our education. I don't even understand why my father wanted a republic. I, on the other hand, wished I could be a queen with a coral, gold crown.

There were several reasons why we loved Hakku al-Khair. First, it wasn't very far from here, only 30km east of the capital. And yet, when we're there, we feel as though we're thousands of kilometers away. Second, people there don't chat about political events or care about Republicans and Royalists. And finally, when you look out into the horizon, the only things you see are the hills, a couple of small mountains, and plenty of grape vineyards. We see animals roaming freely, and children playing out in green spaces. There are no passing cars or screaming truck drivers. Most importantly, our entire time there is spent playing and having adventures in the cave.

We headed back inside, climbing the stone stairs to the fourth floor. Up there, Umi sat in the mafraj,[4] on the southern side of the house. This room gets the most sunlight during the day, which makes it the warmest room in the winter.

As usual, Umi sat on the red floor mattress, resting her back on the numerous pillows in the room, and leaning sideways on a black medka,[5] with a small colourful embroidered pillow on top. With one hand, she held the mada'ah pipe[6] to her mouth, inhaling the charcoal-burnt tobacco. She blew out the smoke through both her mouth and her nose with ease.

None of her girlfriends had showed up to her usual

gathering that afternoon, except for one woman, dressed in a blue gown embroidered with silver threads. In her hand she held a metal plate that she clanked, while she sang in a sweet voice the songs of Ali Al-Ansi:[7]

> *Singing like a bird above the branches of Wadi al-Dour,*
> *your melody opens up old wounds.*
> *What are you thinking stirring up the sorrows of my*
> *heart?*
> *You are neither a lover, nor, like me, have you been forced*
> *to leave your homeland!*

Her voice rose slowly and beautifully, and Umi swayed her head to the rhythm of her friend's voice and the clanking of the plate, all while indicating with her thumb that we be quiet.

We kept silent until they stopped, then Umi took the pipe down from her mouth, looked at us and said, 'So, what's up? It's not the time to give out the Ja'alah[8] yet.'

Raja' smiled and said: 'We don't want candy.'

'So, what do you want then? No good can come from standing there like that.'

Raja' took a step back before gaining the courage to ask. She was six years old, two years younger than me, though she acted like an older sister. Whenever we went with Umi to one of her afternoon ladies' gatherings, Raja' would be the first to greet the guests while I stood shyly behind her.

Raja' said: 'I want to go to 'Hakku al-Khair today.'

Umi tilted her head back, lifting her chin and raising her eyebrows, then pressed her tongue to the roof of her mouth with a 'tttt', in a gesture which we knew meant *No*. Then she looked at me, giving me the look of a judge pronouncing a guilty verdict. A look that silenced me, leaving me without words, until Raja' said the thing that I couldn't bring myself to say:

'I beg you, please, we're about to explode here without

school, and without anything!'

'Have you both lost your mind? People are killing each other and my daughters want to go for walks and wander around after the noon prayers!'

Umi turned to her friend and continued her complaint: 'Have they gone mad? People are fighting and my girls want to go out and stroll around like street girls!'

Raja' burst into tears, sobbing so heavily that she fell to the ground, screaming like a toddler: 'Umi, I can't stand it here, please let us go to Hakku al-Khair!'

'We don't have the car anyway,' Umi replied. 'Your uncle took it yesterday.'

We left the diwan, and I patted Raja' on her back, trying to comfort her. She turned to me and said: 'We'll get there today, we must. Today means today!.. Let's ask Abi!'[9]

We went down to the second floor, and Raja' entered our parents' bedroom. I shouted: 'What are you doing? You know we're not allowed to go in there without asking permission first?'

But Raja' didn't care. She ran to the room, and I followed slowly. At the door, I peeked inside. The sunlight reflected on the wooden cuckoo clock that hung on the bedroom wall, opposite to the golden Qur'an on the shelf. We heard the water running in the bathroom and heard our father recite prayers while he cleansed himself to prepare for prayer. I felt my body tense and my heart race. I was so afraid of what he'd say when he saw that we were in the room uninvited. But when Abi came out, he didn't get angry like I thought he would. Instead, he smiled, simply continuing what he was doing without saying a word.

We watched him apply some oud perfume and then line his eyes with Ithmid kohl.[10] He looked very handsome in his bright white Zanna.[11] I imagined and hoped that one day I'd marry someone as handsome as my dad. He then looked over at us and asked if we could bring him incense. Immediately, Raja' jumped up and rushed downstairs to get some from Umi. Raja' was always faster than me. Perhaps that was the reason Abi preferred her to me, I thought. Or maybe it was just because she was prettier? The irony is that I was named Jamila.[12] I guess the beauty gene skipped me and went to her with her almond eyes, her pitch-black hair, and her confident smile. I often felt bad when I heard people tell her – and not me - how pretty she was. Could this be what others call jealousy?

When Raja' came back, smoke covered her face and all I could see was a pair of legs walking towards us, like something from a horror movie. Raja' began circling Abi to allow the Bukhoor incense to perfume his clothes. She made two rounds, then she began letting the smoke scent her own hair and then mine.

By the time she'd finished, Abi was standing at the top of the stairs, ready to leave. Raja' stopped him: 'Abi, wait, there's something I'd like to ask you.'

'Not now,' he replied. 'I don't want to be late for prayers.'

Abi went down the stairs, but Raja' wouldn't give up, and shouted: 'Can we go to Hakku al-Khair?'

'We don't have the car,' his voice echoed in response. 'Your uncle took it.'

We followed him out to the area in front of the mosque and stopped to lean against the black Abyssinian marble wall. But as soon as the muathin started his call to prayer, 'God is great! God is Great! I bear witness that there's no god but God! I bear witness that there's no god but God!', we got the giggles. We tried hard to stop ourselves from laughing, but we failed miserably. Then Haj Ahmad began yelling at us:

'Disgraceful! You two should respect the Athan. Leave now, go back home, immediately!'

He was right, of course, anyone who laughs at the Athan lacks manners, but we'd remembered a story from last month that made us laugh. One early morning last month, when it was time for the dawn prayer, instead of the call to prayer, we heard the sweetest voice singing: 'All my life, I have feared love, any mention of love, and the injustice love brings to all those it accompanies.' Umm Kulthum's voice resonated from the minaret of Al-Abhar Mosque, and we had no clue why instead of the Athan we were hearing music. A few hours later, we found out that our cousin, known as a prankster, had snuck into the mosque and replaced the Athan tape with one of Umm Kulthum's most popular love songs. Since they started using microphones and loudspeakers, the muathins stopped climbing to the top of the minaret the way they used to. Instead, these days, they just play a recorded tape, turning the volume up to blast the sound in all four directions.

So now, every time we hear the Athan, we remember the prank and laugh.

We didn't leave the mosque, even if Haj Ahmad asked us to. But I tried hard to contain my laughter, so I looked away from my sister. When I looked up, I noticed how the upper balconies of the mosque were made of traditional mud-brick and plaster. It was so beautiful, I finally stopped laughing. And then I thought to myself, how strange are humans? How many times have I been here without looking up?

The worshippers came out, carrying their shoes and their prayer rugs, and Raja' began asking each passerby if they had a car that we could borrow. Some smiled at her, others told her they had a rocket that they could lend us if we wanted to fly into space. Raja' got upset by these replies and was about to give up when Abi saw us and told us a fellow worshipper had agreed to lend us his car. My sister almost burst with joy.

In front of our house, a black Toyota Hilux waited for us with a driver we didn't recognise. Abi greeted him and sat in the front seat beside him. Umi sat in the back and Raja' and I hopped from seat to seat. We drove past al-Abhar Mosque until we reached Al-Sailah, a neighbourhood north of Sana'a, where we saw kids splashing around in small, roadside puddles. After that, we passed Dar as-Sa'ada[13] which people say used to be a military hospital during the time of the Turks that went by the name Agzakhana. After the Turks left, Imam Yahya[14] turned it into a royal palace and his own personal residence, and these days, it was the main governorate building. It was gigantic. Abi told us that when it used to be a hospital, there was a Turkish cleric with a green turban who visited every patient every single day. Umi prayed for the Turkish man, and then recited a prayer for us:

'Our Lord, creator of the heavens and earth, we ask you, generous Lord, to protect us from every evil, as you are the all-powerful.'

'Ameen,' we all responded.

Raja' finally calmed down, and sat in the middle between Umi and me, but she was feeling cramped in her seat, so she asked me:

'I don't like my spot; can I sit in yours?'

'Stay where you are,' I replied. 'You chose your seat and I'm comfortable right here.'

'Come on, I want to sit by the window, please.'

She kept insisting and even kissed my hand twice, but I still refused. So, Umi intervened: 'Jamila, you're the oldest. Be sensible and let your sister look out of the window for a little while.'

I couldn't say no to Umi, so we swapped seats. But I wish I hadn't listened to her. I wish Abi hadn't found a car for us to borrow. If only!

We left Sana'a through the Shagadeef gate, heading north towards the farm, but shortly after, we saw a man standing in the middle of the road with a rifle in his hand. He extended his arm, ordering us to stop. My father asked the driver to obey. But the driver responded: 'There's no need!'

My father shouted: 'Stop! Stop! Stop!'

But the driver refused to. He simply slowed down slightly. Suddenly I heard the piercing sound of a bullet being fired from somewhere, then another noise like someone had banged on a table with a heavy hammer; it almost ruptured my ears. I don't remember everything that happened at that moment, but I remember Umi screaming. And I remember the blood that was flowing out of Raja's head straight on the car seat. I remember Umi crying and screaming and clutching my sister's head to her blood-drenched lap. I remember how just a moment ago, Raja' could not sit still, jumping around with joy, and the next moment she had turned into a still, motionless body. The driver rushed quickly to Al-Jumhouri hospital,[15] and I wished so much that Dar as-Sa'ada had still been a hospital, because it was so much closer. I closed my eyes and, with trembling lips, I recited a verse that my grandfather had taught me: 'And We have placed before them a barrier and behind them a barrier, and covered them so that they do not see.'[16] I hoped that by reciting this verse, we'd arrive at the hospital within seconds and that tragedy would be averted. My grandfather had told us he used to recite this verse on his trips from Sana'a to Taiz to make the journey shorter, and he promised he crossed vast distances in seconds. In that moment, I prayed hard that we would cross Sana'a's streets in seconds and reach the hospital instantly.

I didn't go with them to the hospital; they left me with my cousins in a different neighbourhood of the old city of Sana'a. I was so worried; I couldn't sit still. Every hour, I asked my aunt if there were any developments, and every time she would reply, 'Don't worry, everything is fine.' The next day, when I had no news, and when Umi didn't show up to take me home, as she normally did, and when Raja' didn't come over to play with us, I felt a tightness and a pain in my chest, and I became very anxious. I went into the bedroom and sat alone for two minutes, moving my eyes right and left and then up and down, trying to absorb my fear and the dryness of my mouth, until I suddenly ran away from my uncle's house.

With all my strength, I ran the entire way from Al-Sultan's Garden to Al-Sailah and finally to our house in Al-Abhar. No one followed me. It was as if they hadn't noticed my escape, and when I entered at the house, I found it full of women dressed in black with the sound of the Qur'an echoing all over the place. At that moment, I knew. I searched for Umi, but I couldn't find her on the first floor, nor the second. I finally found her on the third floor, dressed in black, and her eyes were flooded with sadness. Many women wept and mourned around her; I rushed to her, and stayed until her dress was soaked with tears.

Every time I hear the screech of a car's brakes I'm reminded that death walks among us. I know that there is no escaping it, and that we could run towards it at any moment without knowing. But I also know that although Raja' died, she didn't die. In my dreams, Raja' and I still play in the courtyard. Sometimes she wins and other times she loses. I see Raja' whenever I smell basil; I feel her warmth in every cup of tea with cardamom; I hear her voice whenever I sing, and sometimes, I even hear her whisper to me: 'I'm fine.'

Raja' died, but she didn't die. She's always with us.

Notes

1. 11 January 1967, in the Gregorian Calendar.
2. Mum, or mother.

3. In 1962, Republicans, led by Abdallah al-Sallal, overthrew the ruling Mutawakkilite Kingdom of Yemen (North Yemen), leading to a civil war from 1962 to 1970 between the two camps – the Republicans and the Royalists. The Republicans were supported by Egypt's President, Gamal Abdel Nasser. The Royalists, meanwhile, were led by Imam Muhammad al-Badr (ruler of the Mutawakkilite Kingdom) and were backed by monarchies of Jordan and Saudi Arabia

4. A room commonly found in traditional San'ani houses, usually situated in the southeastern side of the house, on the top floor.

5. An armrest pillow.

6. At the time this story is set, Yemenis didn't use hooka (or shisha) pipes. Instead they used a larger smoking pipe called a mada'ah, which used pure, unflavoured, dry tobacco with many pipes, not just one.

7. A popular Yemeni singer known for his beautiful voice, lyrical poems, and interest in the melodies of Yemeni folklore.

8. A bag of sweets, sometimes consisting of raisins, almonds, and sweets, sometimes just sweets.

9. Father or dad.

10. A traditional type of eye cosmetic, typically in the Middle East.

11. A traditional Yemeni attire commonly worn by men.

12. 'Jamila' means beautiful in Arabic.

13. 'House of happiness.'

14. Imam Yahya (full name: Yahya Muhammad Hamid ed-Din) (1869-1948) was the first king of the Mutawakkilite Kingdom of Yemen (aka North Yemen), from 1904 until his assassination in 1948.

15. Al-Jumhouri Hospital means the Republican Hospital.

16. This protection verse from Surah Yasin (36:9) speaks about how Allah can shield people, making them unseen or unreachable to their enemies.

A Photo and a Half-Full Glass

Badr Ahmed

Translated by Raph Cormack

Sana'a, 9am, March 2011

THE AIR IN THE capital was electrified by a high-voltage charge, making the whole city tense and uneasy. The current passed through people's faces and their limbs, leaving behind creased brows, harsh frowns, and anxiously twitching arms and legs. There was loud and frantic activity in the markets, as prices steadily increased with every passing hour – as did the crowds. The trade in fuel and weapons boomed as never before and people talked of nothing but revolution, demonstrations in the squares, and ever-increasing protests.

Al-Hajj Yahya was sitting quietly in his old shop, his two feet raised defiantly in the face of the faltering economy. He was smoking his shisha and obsessively watching the news on the screen of an ancient television set – a model that Toshiba had withdrawn from the market twenty years ago. Most of the shopkeepers in this alley that was crowded with little stalls like his were doing the same thing at this time of day. A few metres from al-Hajj Yahya's shop, a group of women fidgeted under their expansive black cloths. After a long session haggling with one shopkeeper, the cloths left. A policeman waved his kurbash[1] in the face of a young man who quickly ran away chanting 'down with the regime.' Meanwhile, a group of young boys circled around two fighting cocks, someone was painting an advert for a local medical clinic on the wall, and a mentally disturbed man called Saadi wandered the market's alleys barefoot, dressed in filthy rags, unaware of anything happening around him.

Above al-Hajj Yahya's shop, lived Hashim; in a house that was as crumbling and dilapidated as the market itself, just like all the other houses in this ancient part of town. Hashim did not know how long his family had lived in the house; he only knew that he had been born there, and his siblings had too.

Hashim stood next to the window, gazing into the distance with a look of worry on his face. The news broadcasts carried frantic headlines as the wheel of death turned at a terrifying rate, its speed increasing with every second that passed. Although he had his mind set on freedom, Hashim still preferred to shut himself away from everything that was happening. He wanted to obey his parents' wishes; after all, they were old and sick, suffering in this cold house that was heavy with the scents of camphor and gypsum.

He heard his mother's faltering steps coming towards him. She put her palm against her chest, trying to catch her breath. Then, when he turned to face her, she reproached him for standing too close to the window. She reminded him about what had happened to their neighbour Fathiyya last week – she had been hit by a stray bullet when she was standing too close to the window and had died. He replied that the span of our lives lies in God's hands and that everyone's appointed time has been written. She just shook her head in fear and tears welled in her eyes. Elsewhere in the house, Hashim's father coughed as he conducted a conversation with nobody, a habit he had picked up since retiring from his job in the ministry of transport ten years ago. His mother told Hashim, as she did every time she sensed he might be thinking about leaving the house, that she would die if he ever left her because she could not possibly live a single day without him. Her tears fell, her breathing became faster and she pressed her hand down harder into her chest. He moved towards her and embraced her head in his arms, then pressed it to his chest. He swore on all that was holy that he would not leave the house and he would never leave her. The voice of his father in another room got louder, he cursed and screamed until a coughing fit finally silenced him.

Years ago, his mother's anxieties had provoked in Hashim a desire to travel to Libya and settle down there. He had confided this secret in his friend al-Shaybani who, in turn, passed it on to Hashim's mother – no-one could ever figure out whether it had been with good or bad intentions. She became convinced that al-Shaybani was telling the truth when she saw her son hanging up pictures of Gaddafi on his walls and reading the books that the Libyan embassy clandestinely distributed among the Yemeni youth. Before that, he had fantasised about going to Iraq and joining the ranks of the resistance. And before that, it was southern Lebanon. But every time al-Shaybani had done the same thing and every time Hashim's mother stood firmly in his way like the ancient Jabal al-Ta'kar,[2] preventing him from realising his dreams. Each time he capitulated to her sobbing and weeping, giving up all he had resolved, never knowing how his mother had discovered the secrets he had kept hidden in his chest. And each time he surrendered to his parents, he lost another life that he had imagined in vivid detail.

Whenever he had to abandon a new dream, he would drag himself to his bookcase and stand in front of it for a long time, lost in the intoxicating world that the books created inside him. He was always compelled to suppress his own desires; his life went on like this for at least 30 years. He knew that he was his parents' only son and he was the one who had to stay with them, take care of them, and support them. This naturally meant that he had to give up his own desires – at least all of those that would take him outside the country or even outside the house. In the face of all this, Hashim trampled his freedom-loving self under the sole of an iron boot and sacrificed himself to his parents' desires.

But that day... things were different. The flames of revolution were burning most powerfully just a few hundred metres from his house. There was no need to cross any borders or to traverse deserts and jungles to find it. The revolution was right there... It was so close that he felt the heat radiating from its ovens. Chants and banners climbed high into the air. The portents of a new dawn appeared on people's faces and patriotism flowed through their veins like adrenaline. There were slogans written under pictures of people with ugly faces and black, rotten teeth, calling for their downfall. Their paper thrones trampled under the feet of the revolutionaries. With every day that passed, the spotlight on the country grew ever wider as the rats, the thieves and the cold itself tenaciously resisted its light and its heat. Malevolent fingers danced over triggers and those faces with black, rotten teeth armed themselves with foolish smiles as they toured television studios, delivering rambling speeches to the outside world.

His mother's mumbling woke him from his thoughts. She begged him to say a prayer seeking refuge from Satan and to wear the talisman that Yosef the Jew had given them many years ago. When she visited Yosef, complaining about the boy's insomnia and his constant desires to leave the house or even the entire country, he had told her that this amulet would ward off demons and the whispers of Satan.

He hugged his mother's head closer to his chest, then kissed her and promised her once again that he would never leave but told her he had no need of Yosef's talisman. She turned her eyes up to look at him and an ocean of tears welled up inside them, waiting for the right moment to escape. Hashim could not help but shake his head as he told her, calming her worries: 'Okay. I'll wear it and never take it off.'

She gently slipped out of his embrace and walked over to a set of shelves, from which she took down a triangular piece of leather and cloth, covered in a layer of dust. His mother carefully rolled up his sleeve and tied the amulet to his right hand. While she was busy putting it on, he stared out of the open window where, in the distance, the sky filled with black smoke and the sound of bullets reverberated. He heard his father coughing in the other room before he started to sing a Sufi melody in a voice so sweet it made him sad. His mother quickly shut the window and drew the curtains, taking Hashim by the hand and leading him back inside.

*

In the morning, Hashim left the house with the taste of his mother's coffee still in his mouth, filling him with joy. No one in Yemen could make coffee like his mother, no one could pick out and roast the beans like she could, and no one loved coffee as much as her. Despite her doctors' constant advice to give it up, she always started her day with a large cup of it and ended it with an even larger one, interspersing them with countless other cups. Her unchanging refrain ever since her battles with the doctors had begun was: 'As long as my heart is still beating, it's fine.'

Hashim said *salams* to al-Hajj Yahya as he passed by, trying not to bump into the madman who kept standing in his way, mumbling something incomprehensible. He crossed the alley and headed to the main road, his eyes moving quickly across the scene in front of him: the shop fronts, the faces, the junk sellers shouting through their megaphones, the motorcycle that's just hit a truck carrying onions, the corrupt traffic cop running over to the onion truck and grabbing the driver by his collar, the Saddam Pharmacy on the other side of the road where Dina bought his mother's medicine. Suddenly, al-Shaybani appeared in front of him, looking as if he had only just woken up. He carried a leftist newspaper under his arm and held a metal vessel billowing incense smoke in his hand. Pointing into the distance with the newspaper and speaking in hurried tones, he said that the protest would come past them at any minute. He spoke with more excitement than he ever had before but Hashim still did not take him completely seriously. Al-Shaybani lied as easily as he breathed and Hashim could still remember every single lie he had ever told. There were two in particular that he could never forget... the first came the day after the fall of Baghdad. Al-Shaybani had run through the market telling everyone that the Iraqi army had launched a devastating counterattack and pushed the Americans back as far as Umm Qasr in one night. He swore on everything that was holy and vowed to divorce his wife if it wasn't true (he wasn't married). In the second lie, al-Shaybani insisted, in just the same way as he had before, that he had seen Saddam Hussein appear on one of the satellite channels to deny the rumours of his execution. Every time he lied, he swore, just as he was doing today, on everything that was holy. Thinking about these two old lies, Hashim remembered yet another: when al-Shaybani told everyone sitting in al-Hurriya café that the president's airplane had exploded in the sky above Hadramaut. That particular lie earned al-Shaybani a trip to Sana'a's filthiest prison for an eight month stretch.

Hashim just ignored al-Shaybani and his warnings, giving him a fake smile and freeing himself from his grip. Then he cut back into the crowds, swinging the talisman that was tied so tightly around his wrist that it made his whole arm numb. The shouts of the motorcycle driver, the onion truck driver, and the corrupt traffic cop grew louder. The truck driver pulled a kurbash out from behind his seat and hit the policeman across the head with it. The policeman fell to the ground, blood flowing from his head. A woman screamed. Brakes screeched. Feet ran here and there. As the main street got closer, the sound of bullets became louder and clearer. The smell of burnt tyres rose above the smell of the spice shops.

Hashim's head was spinning, his eyes scanning in every direction. The women in black cloth crossed the road to go past him, leaving behind them a trail of weeping and wailing. Suddenly, he found himself swept away by a stream of human bodies. He tried fruitlessly to escape the chanting torrent of people until he noticed an electricity pole, which he struggled to reach and use as a dam to divert the bodies away from him. For several minutes, he was passed by a constant procession of crowds and chants and flags and patriotic songs. He waited another five minutes until the crowd thinned out and he could leave the safety of his electricity pole to head in the other direction. He saw the pharmacy in the distance, but before he had taken two or three steps in that direction, he felt a strong hand grab him from behind and push him against the wall. It then threw him to the ground and handcuffed him; when he tried to say something, he was silenced by a heavy punch. Someone started to beat him with a kurbash and he saw one of those female figures dressed in dark black throw off the cloth to reveal the snarling face of a man carrying a taser which he pushed into the shoulder of a passerby, whom he then tackled to the ground and violently handcuffed. Another black cloth fell to the floor to reveal another hideous face brandishing a taser, which attacked another person in the street. They were like wolves picking off the stragglers on the edge of a flock. The sound of chants faded away, replaced by the sound of terrified feet.

Hashim's mother's eyes, wet with tears, invaded his thoughts and the amulet pinched his wrist. Groups of hideous faces drove the handcuffed bodies with batons and tasers towards the police trucks parked at the end of the alley. The bodies piled on the back of them, writhing in pain with every crackle from a taser. The wind carried the sound of chanting, gunshots and the sirens of the riot police vehicles into the distance. The scowling faces ceaselessly abused the dignity of

51

the bodies before them. Al-Saadi, the madman, saw what was happening and wept. As he sobbed, he called upon the spirits of his fathers and grandfathers and upon the jinni who he said loved him and had been married to him since he was a child. Then he stepped back, lifted his clothes, took out his penis, and started pissing into the air. He repeatedly gestured towards his exposed member, cursing and swearing at the officers. Then he picked up some stones, now covered in urine, and threw them at the police, swearing even louder. By the time the police got to him, he had taken off all of his clothes and was standing there completely naked. They beat him and dragged him to the floor, as he cursed them and their mothers. He was thrown before the feet of a man with a thick moustache and black, rotten teeth. This mustachioed man pushed down on his face with a steel-capped boot and thrust a taser between his legs several times. The madman screamed and the madman wept. As he screamed, the officer with the thick moustache and black, rotten teeth laughed. The bodies were piled onto the back of the police trucks which then moved down the side streets towards oblivion.

*

Hashim can still remember that raging flood of voices and bodies. He can still remember the cracks of the whips on his body and the screams of pain that filled the place. They all pierced the depths of his heart like a jagged knife.

Handcuffed, with his eyes blindfolded, he was thrown onto the cold earth. The air was filled with the smell of blood, bodies, and rotting. Suddenly he heard al-Shaybani's voice, screaming in pain and terror. He was begging them, for God's sake, to stop the beating. He begged them by the Quran, on their mothers' and fathers' lives, on the life of the president himself. He swore that his hands and arms were broken, that his heart was weak, he appealed to their children and their mothers, but still their whips cracked down on al-Shaybani's bones.

More feet marched up to the place where they were being kept. Seconds later, the sounds of whips cracking and people screaming for mercy renewed. Hashim held his breath, waiting for the whirlwind to descend. His heart beat faster and he heard his mother's voice calling out to him. His limbs froze as the storm approached and raged across different parts of his body. He felt a huge explosion inside his head then he tasted blood in his mouth, his head span, a blow cracked down on his collar bone, three blows hit his shoulders, and one of the men kicked him in the face. Numbness enveloped his body and the voices faded away, replaced by a distant whistling sound.

He found himself back in the reception room of his house, the rays of sunset streaming in through the open window and the unmistakable scent of Arabic perfume filling the space. Mustafa Mahmoud[3] was looking out from the black and white television screen, presenting his TV show *Science and Belief*. Suddenly, the voice of the madman ripped him out of this dream, moaning in pain and anguish and calling out in tears for Ahmed Ibn Alwan and a host of other Sufi saints whom no one besides him knew. The last voice that Hashim heard was al-Shaybani loudly insisting that he was an officer in the army and begging the police to leave him alone. The hurricane of blows came back around and Hashim's body went limp. He tasted his mother's coffee in his mouth and heard the sound of his father reciting the Quran as he did every morning after dawn prayers. His eyes grew dark and he surrendered to the numbness. He surrendered totally...

★

As the cold set in, he woke up to find himself alone on the floor of a dark, disgusting cell, teeming with insects. He stared into an endless sea of black and imagined himself floating on a wooden raft through the outer reaches of space. As he felt the damp walls around him, he remembered the clay walls of his bedroom which had been eaten away by the humidity. He remembered his mother. He remembered his father and his constant noises. Al-Shaybani's shouting and begging reverberated in his head, alongside the crying and weeping of the madman. Pain set in across his body and he moaned, sitting up and leaning his back against the wall. His limbs felt heavier and moving them was more painful than before.

He heard the heavy tread of feet in the empty corridor outside. As the sound came closer and became clearer, Hashim's heart beat harder. The door of the cell swung open violently, a torch shone around the corners of the small room before settling on Hashim's face for a few seconds. A fierce shadow approached him, smelling of tobacco and sweat. This shadow mumbled something and spat to the side. Then, it made way for two strong hands to grab Hashim and drag him out of the cell on the ground towards some unknown destination.

*

In a room filled with the smell of alcohol and sweat...

A bald officer with a hooked nose sat behind a wooden desk that was piled high with papers. He noisily played with a set of keys as he examined Hashim's features with tired, bulging eyes. He scratched his chin and the back of his head. Then he opened three buttons of his sweat-soaked shirt, rolled up his sleeves, took off his silver watch and carelessly threw it onto the desk. He twisted the large ring which took up a sizeable part of his ring finger, leaned back, and crossed his arms in front of his chest. The picture hanging on the wall distained everyone in the room with its condescending look and fake smile. A glass filled with foamy amber liquid was waiting next to the officer. He picked it up, emptied half of it down his throat, then slammed it back down on the table. He wiped his mouth with a tissue that he threw unthinkingly into a corner. He got up, sat on the edge of the desk, and wiped his nose for no particular reason. The officer then picked up some sheets of paper which he waved in front of Hashim's face. Hashim stared at the yellowed pieces of paper for some time but he could not understand what was written on them at all so he turned towards the officer quizzically. The policeman cursed him and insulted him, then showered him with question after question – an unending stream of idiotic questions during which he also informed him that the interrogation was being filmed. Hashim replied to any question to which he knew the answer or which he understood, but they were unceasing. The stupider and more ridiculous the questions, the more resentful Hashim grew. He found himself shouting right in the officer's face: 'Why am I here?'

The officer moved towards him and stood directly in front of him, staring right into his eyes. He took a piece of paper in his hand and said: 'Why are you here? You really don't know?'

The Hebrew words that Yosef had written on the amulet tied to his arm were a clear giveaway. Foreign infiltrators were supporting the protests and there were very suspicious links to countries outside Yemen. This was all Hashim could make out from the officer's tirade. He heard al-Shaybani's voice hidden away somewhere; it was faltering and mixed with tears. The words faded in Hashim's mouth and the deep wound in his forehead became enflamed and started throbbing. He supposed he had got it after the officer had slapped him with a huge bundle of papers that he had taken from the desk while he was frantically asking him: 'How much did they pay you to protest?'

He tried to deny everything. He swore on anything he could think of. He tried to convince the officer that he was just going to the market to buy his mother's pills and had found himself in a protest totally by accident. The officer snorted and slapped him very hard four times before dragging him across the floor by the hair. The officer cursed Hashim's mother and rammed his thumb into his wounded forehead, wiggling it sadistically, then spat in his face. After this long, humiliating ordeal, Hashim's heavy feet managed to carry him outside, still blindfolded. The sound of bullets rose in the distance, a fan whirred somewhere close by, and the madman sang a sad Sufi melody, his voice sadder and more tearful than it had ever been before.

In the cell, a fever suddenly came over Hashim and violent chills began to make his limbs shake. He curled up into a ball and saw strange visions of the smiling police officer crossing a lake of tears. He saw his mother praying in the morning, her palm on her chest and the tears shining in her eyes. He saw his father sitting in al-Hajj Yahya's shop, the old man running his fingers through his white beard. He gave free rein to his wanderings and hallucinations. He heard two heavy feet stomping ceaselessly on the roof of their run-down little house. He heard the bald officer laughing louder and louder. The picture in the interrogation room smiled a giant smile then vomited blood from its mouth. His whole body throbbed and he strained his eyes to look around him before sinking back into his pain and his fever.

*

Darkness enveloped the scene again...

Pain shot through his body, the taste of his mother's coffee filled his mouth, and the blood drained from his veins, in its place flowed a strange and unidentifiable mixture of anger and degradation. He felt dirty and unnameable. He felt like he was nothing. Then his mind turned to his right arm. The amulet was no longer there, though the numbness that it had produced still lingered. The sound of screams got louder. Heavy footsteps moved around, doors were opened, others were slammed shut, curses echoed through empty spaces, different voices intertwined and mixed, Hashim's wounds throbbed as different thoughts rushed through his head. The door of his cell swung open. There was nowhere to hide today. The two heavy feet stood in front of him, dragged him out, and put him in front of another officer.

He lifted his eyes to look at the wall. The picture was still looking down on him with a supercilious expression and a sarcastic smile.

The office was crowded, stinking of sweat and aftershave. The picture on the wall staring with scorn at everyone sitting in the room. As Hashim looked around, he saw a bottle wrapped in a page of a foreign newspaper, a cup filled with foamy amber liquid. The fat officer lifted the cup and drained its contents, screwed up his face for a few seconds then burped into Hashim's face. The officer circled Hashim several times, scrutinising his features. Another round of pain and humiliation began, at the hands of this officer. He was tied to the metal rings that were fixed on the wall; he could not stop his limbs from shaking and could not hold back his tears. The policeman's sadism was unbearable but as the officer rained down blows upon him and blood flowed from his nose, he heard his father's voice calling him. As he screamed during the interrogation, Hashim's soul was filled with the smell of coffee. He did not listen or pay attention to the yellowed papers being waved in his face. He just smiled as his interrogator shouted and pelted him with anything that lay on his desk. Al-Shaybani started screaming again. A cacophony of sounds could be heard in the distance: quick footsteps followed by wails of pain. The officer went wild, the bottle was quickly emptied, and the smile on the face of the picture grew and grew, spitting blackness into Hashim's face.

★

Several days of total quiet followed this ordeal. The heaviness and the permanence of this silence made Hashim doubt his sanity. *Am I dead?* he asked himself at first. He looked to the right and to the left, then clicked his fingers to check that he could still hear. He punched the wall with his fist then said a few words to break the silence which filled the space. 'Where have those heavy feet gone?' he asked himself. He hadn't heard them for days. Then he thought, *Why haven't they brought me any food or drink?* It might have been a holiday, he supposed, but there were no official holidays in March.

Perhaps they had just all gone! Maybe everyone had been released! But when? He hadn't heard any doors open. He hadn't heard any voices at all for days. On top of the hunger and thirst, came the cold, the smell of decay, and the insects that swarmed in the dark recesses in much greater numbers than before. Images and memories filled his thoughts, leaving his tormented mind hanging in a state somewhere between consciousness and hallucination. He curled up into a ball and his body began to shiver, as the cold gnawed away at his limbs. His temperature rose and he began to rave deliriously. He called out for his mother; he called out for his father; he called out to the righteous holy men whom his mother beseeched every time she felt a twitch in her eyebrow and whom she often visited with his grandmother to light candles when he was still just a boy.

He kicked at the cell door and unwanted memories flowed into his head; he pictured the trips he used to take to the village, riding on his uncle al-Muhaya's mule. He heard the sound of knocking on metal doors coming from outside the cell and struggled to shake the chains of fever and weakness off his body. He pulled himself up onto his knees and tried to listen. The sound of banging got louder, moving from one cell to another. The whole place rang out with the sound of banging on metal. He kept on kicking the door of his cell with his weak foot. As the noise grew, so did the feeling of weakness in his body. He stepped back, letting the noise inhabit the space that had once held him. An image of the officer appeared before him, pushing down on his face with his polished black boot. Suddenly, he heard sounds coming from a direction they had never come from before. He managed to get to his feet with some difficulty, weighed down by incredible weakness, and put his ear against the door to listen. The noises were coming his way and the thuds of footsteps were getting louder, accompanied by banging against the metal doors. Then the clank of doors opening; then screams. Hashim backed up against the wall, terrified. The feet were moving his way. He began to pray as his body shook in fear. He felt sure that death was coming for him. His life played in front of his eyes like a film reel. All the while, the feet got closer; the banging got louder, the taste of coffee filled his mouth and the sound of his father's warnings filled his head.

His hands searched the ground looking for anything to defend himself. He crouched into a corner, waiting for the unknown person who was bringing these noises with him. The banging reached his cell door. He pushed himself as far back against the wall as he could and curled up his body as tightly as possible. The bolts on his door fell to the ground and it swung open, letting in a gust of cold, dusty air and rays of dazzling light. His throat dried up and his words died. He felt his heart almost break free from his chest as a human body blocked out the light that was streaming into his cell. Another body entered, followed by another. One of them said, with clear excitement:

'There's someone in here!'

His eyes widened in terror. One of the bodies stepped forward and a slender hand reached out towards him. It took him by the wrist as another one of the bodies said with enthusiasm: 'You are free to leave.'

He remained still and silent, not quite understanding what was happening. The voice shouted again, with the same enthusiasm.

'Come on, you're a free man.'

The two hands helped him stand up. He gingerly took his first steps towards the exit. He found himself in a corridor, standing under bright shafts of light and squinting at what was around him. The doors of the cells were open, the locks and bolts had fallen away and were lying on the floor. The passage was crowded with the frail bodies of other prisoners. Other doors began to open and other faces emerged, heading to their appointments with the light and with freedom. He saw bright young faces carrying pickaxes and hatchets to hack away at the last remaining locks on the doors. He stepped out barefoot onto the ground that was no longer cold under his feet and into the corridor that was no longer dark. He passed by the interrogation room to find the door open. He stood in front of it, peering inside to see the papers strewn across the floor and the furniture broken. His gaze fell on the picture frame, which was leaning, face against the wall, shattered. Around it, surrounded by other debris, he saw pieces of broken glass. A faint smile appeared on his face as he crossed the threshold, continuing his journey... to the outside.

Notes

1. Originally a word used for a long, Ottoman-era whip, which can now be used to describe modern-style whips or police batons.
2. A mountain just south of the city of Ibb, which is itself about 120 miles south of Sana'a.
3. Mustafa Mahmoud (1921-2009): a popular Egyptian science writer, broadcaster and author of books of philosophy, science and religion.

Questions of Running and Trembling

Gehad Garallah

Translated by Laura Kasinof

This is not a true story. When you want to tell the truth, you end up stumbling through lies. Not because you want to, but because you're incapable of narrating the small details and that makes you exaggerate every so often. You want your story to be seen, so you add a bit of colour, even if you're unable to give it the attention it deserves. I don't know if this will seem important to you or not, but what really matters here is that a girl decided to run.

My mother is a fearful woman. She ties her hair to the back, and then twists her head around to get a good look at herself in the mirror. She does a double take. She is worried about leaving the house with a poorly tied braid.

My mother is a fearful woman, and when you're a daughter, you cannot help but hold your palms outstretched: you will either catch your mother's fear and become another version of her trembling self, or you will let it go, secretly, and claim that your new-found peace of mind is not something you intended. Then your life may be troubled, but you can still reach a state of burgeoning serenity, for all those bruises it's left you with along the way – they weren't all terrible. Doesn't your steadfast courage confirm that her fear has finally begun to slip away, you wonder.

My mother looks at me. She is wrapping her head in a dark veil, hiding the scrutinised braid. Like other mothers in this city, she hates missing an opportunity to give a lecture. She must always be talking. Her words must be cold, able to strike close to the heart in an instant. This is how city mothers think they can control their daughters' virtue. She is ranting as usual as she puts on her socks. She talks about how we must wash the carpets a second time. She draws a circle in the air to indicate just how large the spot on the carpet is. 'Look at it.' I can't see a spot.

She continues her rant without missing a beat. Do I recall the dreadful amount of dust found on top of my dresser? She describes the wonderful and obedient girl next door, who never ceases to amaze her with her skills in the kitchen – or with her silence. Then suddenly, she has a new theory that explains domestic life: that a woman is known by the way she arranges clothes on the clothesline. She takes off towards the door, spry as a goat, and points to the narrow alley in front of our home.

'Look at this,' she says. 'Is this the laundry of a serious woman?' Her tone is righteous. Evidence has proven her theory correct.

My mother goes back into the room to get her bag, but with less vivacity than before. I don't know when she finds time to come up with all the things she spits out at me every time our eyes meet. Does she plan it all at night when we think she is sleeping or does she just make it up as she goes along? Her manner of speaking amazes me. How does she jump from one topic to the next so seamlessly? Everything she says flows together undisrupted. It's incredible.

She pokes me with her finger. 'We're late.' I follow her like a puppy.

My mother slips her feet into her elegant leather shoes. They have held up well, as if they were a recent purchase. She moves her feet shyly, like she's softening up the soles. I know she enjoys the way her feet look, but she is afraid that I will think she's acting like a teenager if she stares at them for too long. According to my mother, there are certain stages in a woman's life when she is allowed some mirth and vanity, while it's unbecoming for one of us to indulge a pleasure outside the designated age bracket. Such a woman lacks self-possession and piety. Thus, my mother does not give herself much leeway when it comes to her emotions. She is careful that her actions fall in line with what it means to be a mature and respectable woman.

I also braid my hair like she does and put on my shoes. My mother does not like my trainers. Often, she tries to stop me from wearing them by hiding them and claiming to have no idea where they are. Or she will buy more ladylike shoes in my size and place them on the shoe rack exactly where I place my shoes, thinking I won't notice. She says my choices are unwise. Why would I buy running shoes? I am too old to be running around.

'In this city, women don't run.' I feel like I'm being suffocated.

Our steps are measured as we make our way. We walk long distances without ever deviating from our path. I observe my mother's pace as she walks ahead of me. Lithe, diminutive and anxious. It seems to me as if she walks like she is afraid of falling off a narrow ledge. I'm left wondering if she has some kind of secret course she follows whenever she leaves the house. Her steps seem to follow a set of rigid guidelines.

I try to have a little fun, and I branch off towards the middle of the street. I stick my foot out so that it's in the path of oncoming cars. I consider the vehicles and their ability to navigate tight spaces, leaving clouds of dust in their wake. How are cars able to do this? How are they able to drive so fast through the city's busiest neighbourhoods without annoying anyone, whereas I cannot even run outside? I don't understand how my feet are more dangerous than cars.

With this thought, my anger rises and my pace quickens, causing the ends of my abaya to stir up waves of dust like a fluttering bird. My mother notices. She pulls me towards the wall. A cold darkness sets in around us.

'When there is the right amount of light and darkness, then you have the perfect shadow,' she says.

I don't argue. I just stay silent.

My mother always says things that make me want to scream, laugh, or just cry. But as a person gets older, they learn how to keep their own counsel and protect their feelings from the sting of others' words. And so I conceal my true thoughts. She says her piece and I say mine. But she doesn't begin to understand me. She doesn't get that an everlasting shadow is the perfect breeding ground for mould. At times, I'm glad that my mind is able to refuse what my heart desires. Other times, I hasten to ask God to forgive me for what I've kept secret.

'Mothers know everything,' she says.

I smile like a sly fox. What is it exactly that she knows?

My mum stops to adjust my niqab, pointing at my eyebrows which have escaped their dark cover. She scolds me for my negligence and reminds me that I am no longer a child. I cannot use ignorance as an excuse.

'Aren't we going to run?' I ask.

My mother doesn't understand why I'm asking this now, specifically. She often tells me that I open my mouth at inappropriate times and that I throw around empty words. When I was younger, she told me that even the wisest words become nonsense when uttered at the wrong time.

And yet, I thought this was the appropriate time to speak nonsense.

'Aren't we going to run?' I ask again.

'What do you mean?'

'It's like this. We move our feet like this – quickly.'

'You're an idiot.'

She grabs my hand and proceeds to lead me down the street. We go on forever. The streets are like a maze without end. I wonder where we are and where she is taking me. Wouldn't it have been better for us to take public transport, like we usually do? I look around and see houses like massive barricades, glued together, side-by-side, as if they are trying to prevent anything from getting through. I feel like the city is conspiring against me. As a child, I used to love walking through the city, but now I've come to hate it. I used to love the city because it felt like a place of endless possibility. But now I've discovered that what the city offers is nothing like what I thought it would be. I hate it here. Sana'a is no longer anything but blocks that don't fit together properly. Stones sprout up from the earth and vegetation disappears amongst the dreary brown. Each alleyway is spoken for, every inch of the city, every street bears the name of whoever owns it. These streets hold everything: conversations, moments of respite, whole lives, as well as the dreams that Sana'anis hide under the cobblestones each night for fear of what the walls will reveal.

You look around the city and all you see are people scrambling about. They leave their homes because inside they can't breathe, and then they return because outside it's the same. Their faces are devoid of life, yet their feet could weave the most impressive tales. All the while, their children must learn that they cannot hold anything too tightly. On these streets that will only weigh you down, you'll never see a woman laughing. There is a strict set of rules for how to get through your day and it's imperative that you review them each morning – or else expect trouble.

When I describe our city, my mother says I exaggerate. And no wonder. Deep inside, we often assume that the cries of those in pain before us are exaggerated, even if we feign sympathy.

I stop. My mother continues to grip my hand. She tries to pull me along. I refuse to move.

'Where are we going?' I ask. She doesn't reply. She stands unmoved.

My mother always has an answer at the ready. It's like she keeps her replies on scraps of paper hidden in her bra and pulls them out whenever she has to deal with a complaint. But this time she stops and doesn't say anything. I even feel her hand start to loosen its tight grip. She is lowering her defences. Has my simple question caused her to waiver?

I regard her with apprehension.

'Really, where is it that we're going?'

My questioning becomes relentless.

'Where?!'

People notice my voice growing louder. She yanks me towards her and covers my mouth with chapped hands.

'I don't know.'

My mother is a fearful woman – I realised that a long time ago. It was the damage she carried around like baggage, her brokenness. She would tremble, but then deny it afterwards. I saw it in the way she combed my hair, how she held the broom as she swept, and how her fingers shook when she stuck a needle into my father's shirt. Her fearfulness was closing in on me. Life becomes limited when you only gaze at the horizon through a narrow window.

And so I've always wanted to run. I wanted to escape those quiet, anxious tremors, escape everything that put limits on my life. As a child, I used to run as if something was chasing me. Then running became a desperate attempt to escape from myself, an illusion in which a bird thinks that walls are a part of the sky so it doesn't die of grief. When I was younger, I told my mother that I could be a runner. I closed my eyes and imagined my feet dashing through the air. My mother pinched me. 'The reason a house's columns do not collapse is there are women inside who never close their eyes.'

When I turned eleven, I lost my permission to run. My mother was waiting for me to come out of school, hiding behind a wall. She was there to teach me dignity. She snatched my hand and I tried to escape her hold.

'There, to the school gates and back. That's your only route.'

I begged her to let me run. She tightened her grip.

'A respectable girl keeps her breasts firm.'

After that, my pace became more controlled so that no unexpected movements would cause my breasts to bring unwanted attention: anger or desire. It would be indecent for any bouncing to expose that I was a woman. What shame! It was up to me to pretend there was nothing on my chest through calm, calculated movements. I've been fairly successful at not drawing attention to them. Even when my mother was too busy to pick me up from school and I would allow myself to run, sprinting with an unbridled passion, I would use my hands to hold down my small breasts until I reached home.

'Run... run your heart out...,' my mother says now abruptly. 'These narrow alleys will swallow you up once you exceed their speed limit. And when you finally stop, you'll be either insane or a harlot. No one will believe otherwise. Not one person will say this is just a girl who wanted to test the limits of her world.'

I realise that mothers know everything. My hand slips from hers and she walks away. I follow her and this time I feel like she knows where she's going. She picks up her pace and it is me who trembles inside.

The houses around us, which I at first regarded as obstacles, are now transformed into paper planes. From inside the homes, we can see women gazing out at us. They are clapping, urging us onward.

It is then that we come to a large iron gate and enter through it into a walled yard.

We can run here, as it's a protected space. There's no one

to inspect my backside if I decide to soar with the wind. It's a place where going through life does not elicit suspicion or worry. Here we are free.

Even then, my mother looks around to assure herself that no one is following us.

She kicks off her shoes and rolls up her abaya. With her finger, she draws a line across the ground and shouts: 'Let's race!' I draw closer to her. I crouch down and steady myself.

'One…two…three…'

We run.

Our eyes fill with tears like oases in the desert, and all that surrounds us are graves.

Shadows of Sana'a

Maysoon al-Eryani

Translated by Katherine Van de Vate

'WAKE UP! WAKE UP! It's nearly dawn!'

'All right... all right... God give me strength...' grumbled Sarim.

After a fierce battle with the devil, he got up and performed the shaf' and witr prayers, followed by the dawn prayer.

Sarim was a young man of 32. Most of the time he wore a tunic and shawl and carried a dagger. He made sure his tunic was short, since he was extremely devout and thought a short tunic was more virtuous.

Sarim and his younger sister Ghasiq lived in Sana'a's old quarter in an old-fashioned house that had belonged to their grandfather. They had been born at the same time of day, in the same place, and had a common father, which meant that their fates were forever entwined. They shared the house with two companions, Idris and Lahab, but Sarim was the only human among them. Each day he awoke to prepare their breakfast and eat with them, carefully limiting the amount of salt he used. When Shaikh Idris asked why the food wasn't salty enough, Sarim would retort: 'Because you're a jinn! Jinn don't eat salt, do they?!'

Lahab would rage and storm until flames spurted from his ears. 'Look here, you, we're jinn, not devils!' Sarim, Ghasiq and Idris would burst out laughing till Sarim clarified: 'I was only joking. I'm trying to keep my blood pressure down.'

Every morning Sarim went out to open up his little stall in the salt souk. The shop was colourful, filled with every sort of precious stone – Iranian emeralds, Yemeni carnelian, turquoise, amber, and silver with Iranian, Turkish, and Bahraini filigree. The shop was the favourite place of his pampered little sister Ghasiq. She would wander through it, swaying from side to side, gazing at the gems in astonished delight as if seeing them for the first time. She had amber eyes and long blonde hair, a radiant complexion and cheeks like summer apricots, while necklaces of blue sapphire adorned the front of her sparkly dress, which was the colour of the sky.

The salt souk would fill up with all sorts of people, from old women wrapped in colourful scarves to young men browsing, horsing around, or selling water. A teenager moved through the crowd offering chilled raisin juice from a big copper pot on his back, secured to his waist and shoulder by ropes. As he cried, 'Cool down! Cool down!', he handed a cup of juice to an old man sitting outside the Great Mosque. They seemed to be in cahoots, since the old man never requested the juice. Afterwards, the boy would disappear into the maze of alleys, still crying 'Cool down! Cool down!'

When it was time for the noon prayer, Sarim – Shaikh Sarim, that is, for he was an important man – would lock up his shop and head for the mosque before having lunch with his friends whose shops adjoined his. Afterwards, they would all head back to the market to buy qat, that accursed plant... But Sarim always refused to accompany them, muttering: 'If you want to keep the friendship and affection of the righteous jinn, you have to stay on the straight and narrow!'

Sarim always returned to his shop late in the afternoon, when the markets of old Sana'a once again hummed and people flocked there to buy salt, wool, grain and other goods.

Every day Laila passed by him on her way home from the university, where she was in her second year of studying English. She was head-over-heels in love with Sarim and never failed to come to the salt souk. Laila was slender and modest, but she was also a lively girl, cheerful and chatty. Though her conduct was beyond reproach, she was not exactly Sarim's type; she lacked, for example, the purity of Ghasiq. Sarim wanted a girl who was infallible, whose hair, gait and behaviour not even the wind could ruffle.

'How are you today, Shaikh Sarim?' Laila would enquire, and averting his gaze, Sarim would mumble in response: 'I'm well, young lady. You'd best be on your way.' As she left, Laila would quietly croon the words of Faia Younan:[1]

'You'll be mine if you love my homeland as I do'

'I'll be yours if my people return to their homeland...'

Laila repeated this routine every day. After two years, Sarim's heart finally softened and he began looking forward to her visits, although his rational mind as well as the people around him would never accept her. But who can resist the heart forever? Who can withstand the thorns of longing and the eyes' allure?

One evening, Shaikh Idris and Lahab got into an argument about Laila and Sarim.

'How long is this human going to hang around our son? Till when?' Idris demanded. 'Everyone in the market is gossiping about them. May God save us from her evil!'

'Are you ordering us to exile her?' Lahab asked.

Sarim's heart trembled. Pretending to be headed for the toilet, he got out of bed and said:

'Let me sleep! I'm exhausted, and you're keeping me up.'

Looming over Sarim with all the gravitas of his three thousand jinn years, Shaikh Idris said sternly: 'This girl is not acceptable, and that's our final word on the subject, so don't you dare give her another thought. You're my son; I chose you from all of humankind and the jinn, and I raised you myself after your parents died. It's useless trying to trick me, and if you try to disobey me, I'll incinerate you both on the spot. It is I who will choose you a suitable bride. Do I make myself clear?'

'Yes, perfectly!' replied Sarim. 'I'll do whatever you want! Don't give it another thought – there's nothing to worry about.'

Yet Sarim was incredibly sad. He returned to his bed, his heart shuddering like a mother whose child has been snatched away. Clutching his chest, he wondered: *What's happening to me? What are these emotions crushing my heart? I feel like I'm suffocating or going crazy! I know God's Book by heart and I'm the chief justice for both the jinn and mankind. Why, oh why, can't I control my heart?* Trying to ignore the lump in his throat, he recited God's praises until he fell asleep.

'Wake up! Wake up! It's nearly dawn!'

'All right, Laila, right away!'

Ghasiq's face froze and she clapped her hand over Sarim's mouth lest he repeat himself and be overheard. But Sarim was just as mortified. *'A'udhu billah min al-shaitan al-rajim!* God protect me from accursed Satan!'

Rising to his feet, he spread out his prayer rug and began to pray at length, as if to postpone facing himself and the rest of the world. After he had calmed down, he fixed breakfast. Though his mood was still dark, he went out as usual to open up his shop. Morning and afternoon passed to their usual tempo as he waited anxiously for Laila to turn up. Occasionally he glanced at the street, especially the alleys from which Laila used to arrive, but in vain.

That difficult day was followed by another and yet another. On the fourth afternoon, Laila finally appeared, accompanied by a friend. As usual, she looked at Sarim, and for the first time he returned her gaze with more than a fleeting glance. Though he felt as if a light, cool rain had fallen on his heart, he turned away as if nothing had happened, and Laila went on her way.

Suddenly, he heard screaming in the street – Laila!

'Ayy! You son of a dog! Damn you!'

Without thinking, Sarim leapt from behind his shop counter and raced towards her. The back of her abaya had been ripped open by one of the boys roaming the market, and her friend was frantically trying to find something with which to cover her so they could make their way home.

Sarim snatched a curtain from a shop doorway and wrapped it around Laila. He struck the boy, who was staring at Laila and mocking her, and they traded blows until people broke them apart.

Sarim shouted at Laila in a fury. 'Get out of here, go home this minute! What are you doing in the street at this hour? It's nearly sundown!'

Distressed at this unjust rebuke from the man she loved, Laila gathered up the fragments of her shattered heart and left.

Sarim headed to the mosque for the sunset prayer, muttering to himself: 'Spare me Your wrath, oh God; save me from this evil!'

He was angry, but not at Laila. He was angry at the boy who had hurt Laila and made Sarim shout at her, angry because the entire souk had witnessed her tears, angry because his heart would not stop pounding. He knew now that he was in love with Laila, though she did not conform to any of his beliefs or to his image of his life partner.

When he reached home after evening prayer, Sarim found more than sixteen jinn kings assembled there. Under the direction of King Idris, they were planning to marry Sarim off to a princess from their world. Sarim was transfixed with astonishment. He was the judge for his people and they held him in the highest esteem. How could such a thing happen so fast and without even asking him?

He pulled off his shawl. Placing it at the feet of his father, King Idris, he fell to his knees, surrendering all his prestige as the king's son and the gateway between humankind and the jinn.

'Father, you know what is in my heart. You see what I cannot see, you hear what I cannot hear, and you know what I do not know. I will do whatever you command, but don't order me to marry someone other than Laila. I've tried ignoring her; I know she's far from ideal and she's not a suitable bride for a king. But her free spirit is like an iridescent butterfly that reflects the glory of God's creation. Is there any heart like hers, any beauty comparable to hers?'

The Red King asked the assembly: 'Who is he talking about? How dare he openly defy us when we are so much older and more important than he is?'

King Idris was the leading king among the jinn. He could not tolerate the Red King's rebuke of his beloved son, Sarim, on whom he relied wholeheartedly. Banging his staff on the ground, Idris ordered Sarim to leave the city and forget Laila, the woman he loved, forever.

Meanwhile, Ghasiq was eavesdropping behind the door. When she heard the king's decision, she could no longer control herself. Seizing a pair of scissors, she stormed into the gathering, chopped off her golden hair and let it drop onto Sarim's shawl.

'I am the Princess of Light and Ice, the daughter of fire and rain! I am the night and the daughter of the motherless horse! When my mother died, she bequeathed me my father's fame and lineage. He was the Horseman of the Sun, and were he here today, not one of you would dare to stand upright.'

'I have cut off my everlasting hair to intercede on my brother's behalf. Love is a storm we cannot escape, and everyone has a right to it. This is Sarim, my father's son. Accept the girl and let him try. Opposites attract, and God is the Lord of all opposites. Perhaps she will be his queen – his earth and his sky. Assign a guard to watch her for a year, then meet again and make your decision. Leave the matter till spring…'

At these words, the jinn backed down and King Idris reluctantly rescinded his order. The kings voted their assent, and Idris was forced to accept the situation, though he was heartsick and angry at their public defiance of his orders. He placed his seal on the decision and stormed off.

The King's abrupt departure spoiled Sarim's joy, leaving him with shattered nerves and a painful lump in his throat. Idris was gone for three days, and Sarim could not find him. When Idris returned, he ate his meals but remained as silent as if he were deaf and blind. Sarim tried everything to regain Idris' favour, even abstaining from food until he was near death, but to no avail. Ghasiq told him: 'Don't be sad, brother. He will change his mind, God willing; one day, he may even come to love and accept her.'

Caught between the hammer of love and the anvil of loss, Sarim spent most of his time crying and confiding in God. Idris relented slightly, but he still said nothing and had not a single kind word for Sarim. Truly, the decisions and judgments of the jinn are as sharp as the blade of a sword.

For the remainder of the year, there was an atmosphere of tension in the house. When it came time for the final decision, the kings gathered to question the guard they had placed over Laila. The guard reported that she was a girl of impeccable character, fully deserving of love, whose good deeds were known throughout the ancient streets of Sana'a, even in its smallest alleys. Every vagrant and every passerby expressed their gratitude towards her, and that explained everything…

Note

1. A contemporary Syrian pop singer.

The Girl of the Fountain

Afaf al-Qubati

Translated by Mohammed Ghalayini

IT WAS ONE OF those rainy summer afternoons; the sky above Sana'a was scattered with tufts of clouds that had settled onto the verdant foothills of its twin mountains. The cliffs towered above the city like guards flanking their queen, their slopes adorned with flowering pomegranate and almond trees. The whinnying of horses roused me from my contemplation. The Ottoman Wali's[1] soldiers were parading through the Urdi Barracks courtyard and in among those following it were my mother, my uncle and I. But the outing was cut short when my uncle took us each by the hand and led us away from the crowds and back home.

Our house was one of those buildings that had been in place in the old city since before time was time. A red, twilight glow blanketed us as we bid the sun farewell for that day and chit-chatted on our way to Bab al-Yemen. We had barely settled into our front courtyard after the long walk home when a series of sharp, rapid knocks on the door startled us. My uncle hurried to open the door, but before he could discern who it was, a middle-aged woman in a striped black gown burst in. Her dark skin did not mask the pallor of her

77

face. She kissed my mother's hand, and although I did not understand the language she spoke, her tearful pleas were clear for all to see. My mother calmed her down and, wasting no time, ordered me to get the midwifery kit from the storage cupboard in the east room.

For the first time, my mother was going to take me with her to attend a delivery, with my uncle accompanying us to make sure we were safe as we walked through the shadowy alleys that were now cloaked in the silence of the night. We reached an ancient house on one of the alleyways that housed Ethiopians who came to stay in Sana'a during the hajj season and ended up settling here. There were quite a few of them in that quarter, and many worked in the various travellers' inns throughout the city as porters or stable-hands.

My mother set about delivering the girl's baby. It was going to be a difficult birth. The girl seemed no older than thirteen to me, with a thin and slight body. Her face was that of a child forced by a cruel fate into carrying another child, her body filled before her season had come. I helped my mother with the difficult operation, though I was no older than fifteen myself and still a virgin. Our traditions did not allow this, but necessity overrules convention. Once my uncle had dropped us off, he ran to make it to his shift; he worked in one of the inns as a treasurer, safe-keeping money and valuables for pilgrims and other visitors to the city.

That night was not easy for my mother, and it was close to dawn by the time the girl delivered the baby she was carrying, after relentless toil and countless prayers.

As soon as the dark-skinned girl emerged from her arduous delivery, my mother gave me her baby, a girl swaddled in a white cloth and wrapped in a red wool blanket with yellow stripes. My mother then found a hessian coffee sack and put it on my back so it fully covered my black cloak. 'Wrap the sack around the baby when you leave her,' she said tersely. 'Make sure she isn't eaten by the stray dogs. Wait until one of the worshippers arrives, then put her on the platform surrounding the *sabil* fountain.[2] If she's asleep then prod her until she cries and leave her by the fountain then hide behind the *sidr* tree[3] in the courtyard. Just know this, if you get this wrong, don't bother coming home.'

I was overwhelmed by a wave of terror that crashed on me again and again. My jagged breathing drowned out the night's rushing wind. I was gulping sixty times a second.

It was four in the morning, and the streets of Sana'a were deserted apart from the hungry dogs and the faint light from the lamp in the Abhar Street courtyard.

It was a moonless night. The howling wind and the croaking frogs in the mosque pond made it feel even darker. After a few minutes that seemed like an eternity, I made it to the platform that held the *sabil* fountain and crouched behind it there by the left-hand corner of the mosque, in front of the large wooden gate. The ground was sodden, more mud than dirt, and I barely managed to keep my balance while holding the baby, who was contently suckling on a dried date tied to her delicate wrist.

The minutes passed slowly, tinged with cautious anticipation. As I waited, I realised that my mother had perfumed the sack covering me with myrrh. I wasn't sure why she had done this, perhaps to ward off demons… or more likely to keep the dogs from catching the scent of the baby?

Twenty minutes passed and I heard the clatter of the muezzin's wooden clogs as he ascended the stairway to the minaret. Upon reaching the top, he started his usual recitation in a distinctive and powerful voice with a flourish of *tajwid*:[4]

Glory to Allah, the magnificent
Glory to He who owns the Kingdom of the heavens
Glory to my magnificent lord.

A shiver pulsed through me unlike anything I had felt before, even though I heard the muezzin in our neighbourhood mosque reciting similar prayers every day. The serenity of the scene only struck me when the barking of the dogs died down momentarily. At that moment, I was also filled with happy anticipation of the call to the *fajr* prayer heralding that my return to my mother was near. The end of the muezzin's recitation lulled me into a fleeting nap whose enveloping calm was pierced by the call to the *fajr* prayer.

I took up my position as instructed by my mother and stood alert, awaiting the first of the worshippers to arrive for the prayer while the child's cries grew louder and louder. I fumbled in my confusion and uncovered her face to return the dry date to her mouth to soothe her. A lamp was lit nearby, which was soon accompanied by several others. In the dim light, I noticed the blueness of her tiny eyes and her minute, beautiful features. The few locks she had were light blonde, her black skin intermixed with her blue eyes surprised me and triggered a sense of pity inside me. I held her so close that our hearts beat in harmony. Without hesitation, I knew what I had to do. In a few, quick strides, I was in the centre of the square by the mosque. I looked to the right, towards a big house that was only a few metres away, surrounded by a garden that spanned both sides of a short alleyway. I had to hurry to get there before the worshippers, who were about to leave their houses to make it to the prayer on time. I got to the end of the alleyway and paused by the mud brick wall that surrounded the garden of the big house. I hid under an old berry tree, its branches spread beyond the garden wall and neared the ground offering me generous shelter.

It was barely a few minutes later that I heard the sliding of the bolt on the large wooden door and out came a man wearing a dajla gown of woolen broadcloth, his head adorned by a brown *ammama*[5] and holding a long wooden rosary that I glimpsed as he turned to close the door. I could hear the murmuring of recitations and prayers whose meaning I could not discern. I kept my eyes on him till he disappeared into the darkness. Then I waited a short while before setting about hanging the sack-cloth to one of the berry tree branches. I chose one that was further from the ground. I strapped it well with the belt I had around my waist to form a small cradle and there I placed the child, making sure she had no chance of falling.

I was feeling unsettled and my head was filled with disparate thoughts. I needed to find a hiding place to watch my girl, to be sure that she would be taken in by someone trustworthy. My only option was in a house next door to the big house. It had a narrow corridor leading to a battered wooden gate that seemed to be an entryway for livestock. I strengthened my resolve and went in. As expected, my nose was flooded with the stench of animal droppings in a small pen that housed goats at the end of the passageway. I felt my way to find a mud brick wall and some bushells of dried corn leaning against the wall. I moved one of the bushells and sheltered amongst them where I had a good sightline to the girl through the gaps in the wooden door. Twenty more minutes passed and in that time, the new day started taking its first breaths as the threads of light slowly lifted the dark blanket of night. The dawn chorus of *hazars*[6] filled the garden as the light morning breeze caressed me gently. Suddenly I heard the shuffling of shoes and the voices of the worshippers returning from the mosque, praying and wishing each other health, happiness and wealth on this new day.

The master of the big house came closer and my anxiety increased tenfold as he walked home in his cape, carrying his long string of wooden beads. He reached for a metal key in the pocket of his white woolen cape and started opening the sturdy wooden door. After a few repeated clicks, the bolt gave way to open with ease. He hurried inside and I was simultaneously confronted with shame and the sensation of tears running down my cold cheeks. Had I made an error in judgement? Had my plan failed? I heard the sound of the goats stirring and realised they had noticed me there in the midst of their fodder. I collected my sorry self and quietly opened the door to the pen and swiftly scurried back home while taking in the dawn. The sun was slowly weaving its threads onto the faces of Sana'a's mud-brick houses as their windows twinkled back coquettishly. I had barely managed a few steps when I decided to go back to my girl one last time. I uncovered her dark face and her piercing blue eyes and untied the dried date dummy from her wrist before resuming my journey home.

I emerged from the alleyway of the big house and skirted the big square on the side farthest from the mosque. I used the branches of the *sidr* tree for shelter even though their thorns pricked me. I went on till I reached a very narrow alleyway that opened onto the half-buried domes of one of Sana'a's public baths. I took a deep breath and started running, sometimes jumping, between the domes till I reached an opening leading to our neighbourhood's *miqshama*.[6] It was a large plot at the intersection of five streets. I went so swiftly even the djinn of King Solomon wouldn't have caught me. I ran this fast out of fear of being seen by anyone. I arrived home panting and dripping with sweat and with a sense of foreboding pervading my soul. As I reached the threshold, I noticed that the door was open and realised that my mother had left it ajar for me. I was expecting a slap across my face the moment I went in.

Slowly I climbed the steps to our house, I was spent. Once inside, I could barely sit upright as my mother held me in her arms and embraced me. I cried and said nothing. She asked me, 'Did you put her by the sabil as I told you? Allah will take care of her. Allah takes care of what is his.'

The day that followed was filled by a deep depression that mirrored my night. I could barely eat apart from a small amount of warm milk and barley bread that my mother insisted I have. I spent that day peering through the *mashrabiya*,[8] watching the people going past and hoping for any news of my poor girl. My mother could not abide me in that state and put on her robe adorned with ruby and silver and left the house at noon. I understood that she was attending a celebration for a baby because that's what she wore to those occasions in a *tayraman*[9] belonging to one of Sana'a's richest and most influential men.

My mother was a skilled midwife with a good reputation for creating the qishr coffee[10] for postpartum women, so I wouldn't see her most afternoons. She returned as usual after the last prayer of the day, accompanied by one of the guardsmen from a house she was working at. He bid her farewell with few words and gave her the pouch of rubies and silver that she leant out to women at these occasions. My mother closed the door firmly behind her, getting my attention. Her face was bright as she came into our small room. I had just finished my prayers and my eyes were full of sadness. She smiled as she saw me and announced with child-like joy, 'The fountain girl – God delivered her to the judge's house, the one with the big garden.' My heart jumped with joy as I embraced my mother and finally felt at peace.

Notes

1. A governor or regional administrator in the Ottoman empire.
2. A *sabil* is a water jug or more recently a tap or fountain set beside a road or in a square for drinking, provided as an act of charity.
3. The *sidr* tree, also known as the Jujube, Lote or Christ's Thorn tree, is an evergreen, mentioned in the Quran as the tree at the last boundary before heaven. Yemeni *sidr* honey is highly valued due to its scarcity.

4. The correct pronunciation of Quranic texts.

5. A piece of cotton cloth wrapped around the head, like a turban. Symbolically significant to Muslim men, and common in Iran, Afghanistan and Yemen, as well as North Africa, it denotes authority, strength and honour.

6. A type of nightingale.

7. An allotment in the middle of an urban community, best known for growing radishes, or as they're called in Sana'a, 'qashmi', hence the name.

8. A perforated wooden, oriel window.

9. The uppermost room, or penthouse, of a traditional Sana'ani house.

10. A special type of coffee made from the outer shell of coffee beans, famous in Sana'a and other North Yemen cities, to be drunk by *bnaf* women - those who have given birth within the last 40 days.

Sana'a's Missiles

Gamal Alsha'ari

Translated by Basma Ghalayini

I STAND IN FRONT of the mirror, staring at a face I don't recognise. My beautiful wife has placed a plate full of nuts and sweets on the wooden table in front of it. A well-groomed newlywed stares back at me with freshly moistened skin and a precisely trimmed beard.

I firmly straighten my coat, as I try out different expressions, my newly-capped teeth shining. All that time and effort the dentist spent on them has paid off, just in time for our wedding.

My bride wakes up in time to silently clock my open lips and protruding teeth while I stick my tongue out to make my latest face. She watches me quietly, with her hand over her mouth, suppressing a laugh. I see the spark in her eyes and we go quiet for a second... and then another second... before bursting into a laughter that shakes the universe to its core.

My legs weaken from the laughter; I turn and lean against the dressing table, as my wife, like a luminous aura, adjusts my jacket. She sprays perfume on my neck and places her finger on a small dent under my chin, in a failed attempt to conceal something. She raises her eyebrows and bulges her eyes, to try to hide her exhaustion from the night before, the first night we spent together in one bed.

I turn back to the mirror again and see a small red mark in the shape of her lips where her finger had been a moment before, I purse my lips and stare at her, then wink. We laugh, we all laugh, this is where you need to concentrate and put two and two together, I said that we *all* laugh, I thought the whole city could hear our laughter.

In a flash, before I get a chance to speak, she puts some nuts and raisins in my pocket.

'You were the most exhausting and pleasurable woman last night,' I say.

Her reflection resides in my pupils. Quickly she looks down, trying to hide her shyness, she escapes, and escapes and escapes some more.

It's a tradition in Yemen for the bride and groom to have guests over the day following their wedding. So I have to leave her alone with her shyness and receive the arriving guests, I straighten myself and blow her a quick kiss, as we say goodbye to each other.

I open my bedroom door only to find a mass of people gathered behind it; my father looks pale and depressed, like a mother who's lost her children. My mother the same, as she tries to hide her tears, my brothers and sisters likewise. They stare at me in silent frustration.

As I close the door behind me, my smile turns into a frown and my brow furrows with annoyance as I see a fat tear dangling off my older brother's eyelid. I shout at him and shake him: 'Why are you crying? Why? Look, I'm married! Why are you ruining my joy? Why? Why?'

My mother bursts into tears. Exhaling sharply, she rests her head on the hallway wall. Then I see her slide down it slowly to the floor.

I kneel down to her in shock: 'Why are you robbing me

of my joy?' I ask her disgruntled.

'May God take away the joy in his life, whoever took your joy away from you, son,' she says. 'May God seek redress from whoever did this to you on your wedding day. They took both your joy and ours. How could they! How could they!'

She wails and I cup my head, as I start to spin as all the planets spin around with me simultaneously, apart from Saturn, which seems to be wailing along with everyone else around me.

'I am the groom!' I say, once the planets stop orbiting around me, apart from the Earth, which is still causing me to lose my balance.

'I am the groom, I'm the groom!'

My voices fades.

'The groom...'

My legs can no longer hold me, I collapse in slow motion, only reaching the ground in the time it takes to fall from the Eiffel Tower. I find myself next to my mother, my father kneels down, placing his palms on my head.

'You'll be ok, Son. You'll be ok.' My father has a way with words.

'I'm fine, Dad!' I say, 'My life is so much better now! I've lucked out with my wife, punched above my weight. She was just making me laugh a few moments ago, and spraying perfume all over me!'

I turn to my mother, her cheeks glistening with tears, and, with a puzzled sigh, I take out some raisins from my pocket.

'She's just given me some nuts and raisins,' I stutter. 'My wife is just like you, Mum, loving and tender; she loves me the way you all do!' No one can look me in the eye. Though his back is turned, I can see my father shaking like a volcano about to erupt. My mother is the only one facing me with her sharp exhales, unable to hide her hyperventilating. My eldest brother shamelessly cries in anguish; the exhales get louder, the tears fall faster. I feel the city flooding.

I still don't know why they're crying; I trace my mother's last tear down to her feet, a dark veil falls upon me. I struggle to see through it. All I see is darkness and pain.

Night falls, a beautiful summer evening bringing my bride and I together, a night of dancing like something from *A Thousand and One Nights*. The following morning, I once more close the bedroom door behind me, after a night of her taking care of me.

The same scene greets me: my family assembled behind the door. I throw some raisins into my mouth, one after the other; they slide down my throat, lifeless and alone. Tasteless. I can hear my family's cries, and wonder what's making them so miserable, but find no answer. Ignorant of the cause, I cry along with them in solidarity.

Once more, I enter the same cycle of pain, fear, sadness and bewilderment.

Another day passes with more sobs from my usually strong brother.

It's like waking up every morning at a murder victim's funeral: you're one of the pallbearers and you promise revenge, even though you have no idea who anyone is (the killer or the victim)!

I am curious, like someone wanting to catch up on world news first thing in the morning, but I never get my answer.

Two days, three, a week passes. Every morning they wait behind the door, sobbing. My wife's plate of raisins and almonds is now empty and my parents' eyes are swollen, as if they'd been tortured. My sibling's eyes are puffy.

On the final day, my brother offers to take me and my father for a walk. They don't give me a chance to ask if my wife wants to join us.

I find myself on a fancy chair in an office, daydreaming about my nights of pleasure with my wife. I am oblivious to the details of the conversation taking place around me (my brother and father are talking to the person who received us).

They are busy talking about whatever it is they're talking about, and I am busy with thoughts of her. She's my happiness. I smile as I remember the piece of candy she fed me out of the palm of her hand. My smile widens.

I put my hand in my pocket and feel the last of the pieces she gave me this morning. Her smile passes in front of me, like heaven. My smile widens again.

My thoughts are suddenly interrupted by out host, who I later learn is a psychiatrist.

'He's going through a nervous breakdown,' he says. 'It's triggered a temporary amnesia.'

My wife's image gradually dissolves; her cropped shirt, her bare hands and her neck all disappear. Her image turns into a pencil sketch as her features disperse until all that's left is her smile.

'The only solution is for him to be subjected to a second shock that will make him forget the shock of the wedding night, the night his wife was killed,' the doctor tells my father.

The reels of a videotape turn in my head: a movie, directed, it seems, by a sadist, in which missiles rain down on our wedding venue. I stand helplessly as people stampede around me, their wailing and cries for help crescendo through the hall.

'The bride and some of the well-wishers were killed. Others were injured.'

I remember that sound. It's coming back to me; my ear drum vibrates. The noise swirls around me. I put another raisin in my mouth. I try to swallow it. My eyes burn and I can feel a mix of tears and mucus slide from my nose to my open mouth, nauseatingly salty. I pant heavily, my lungs almost jumping out of my chest. My lips quiver, my eyes squint and my body trembles. When I gasp, I can't swallow it. So I start crying. I weep and I wail.

'Our hearts are burning for you, Son,' my father says.

He looks how I imagine a land would look if it was hit by a magnitude-ten earthquake. He shakes and sobs.

My brother shrinks next to him, crying weakly.

And from the brink of that towering waterfall of sorrow, they lead me, from one gasp to the next. The only difference is this time, I know why.

About the Authors

Badr Ahmad is a writer from Taiz in Yemen. His publications include *Black Rain* (2013), *Between Two Doors* (2018) and *Five Days Untold* (2021), which was translated into English by Christiaan James for *Dar Arab* (2021), and was longlisted for the Republic of Consciousness Award (2022).

Atiaf Alwazir is a bilingual writer, educator, and multimedia artist. Her creative practice ranges from essays, short stories, and poetry to sketches, spoken word, and theatrical performances. Her work explores concepts of identity, sexual trauma, exile, and 'home'. Her TEDx talk, 'The Other Side of Yemen's War' focused on the importance of owning our own narratives. Previous artistic partnerships include SkinMutts, Les Polymorphistes, SpeakEasy poetry collective, and Poetik Rios. You may find her work in publications including *ArabLit Quarterly*, and *Middle East Eye*.

Maysoon al-Eryani is an award-winning poet and journalist from Yemen. She was born in Sana'a. Her publications include *Tricks* (2016), *The Mysterious Side of Paradise* (2013), *Madad* (2010), and *I'll Penetrate the Sky by Lovers* (2009). Her awards include the Tulliola-Renato Filippelli Poetry Prize, Italy (2021), the Maqaleh Prize for Arabic Literature: Poetry (2013). and the President's Prize for Young Poets (2009).

Gehad Garallah is a writer and cultural activist. The Chinese translation of her story 'Lunch' won the Most Popular Story award category in Tilk al-Kesas (These Stories) Award in 2020. Her story 'The Heart of the Last Cat' won second place in the Science Fiction Literature Competition at the House of Culture and Art, Washington DC.

Hayel al-Mathabi is a journalist and the author of 20 books, the most popular of which is *The Elevator in Criticism of Theatre*. He works as Director of the Research and Studies Department at the Yemeni Ministry of Culture.

Rim Mugahed is a short story and article writer, published in various Arabic websites and newspapers.

Afaf al-Qubati is a new writer of fiction. She graduated from Sana'a University's Islamic Studies programme in 2004. She works as a teacher and is a member of the Yemen Story Club.

Gamal Alsha'ari is a novelist and playwright, who works in media as a TV program producer. His novel *Tri Schizophrenia*, published by Yastoron (Egypt, 2017), won the Arabic Creativity Award (Cairo, 2019), and the Arab Council for Culture Grant, AFAC 2016. His play *Battle of the Ages* won the President of the Republic Award for Literature and Arts (Yemen, 2010). His published works include *An Illegitimate Novel* published by Yastoron (Egypt, 2020).

Wajdan al-Shathali is a storyteller and writer. He has a short story collection, *The Exposed Part of the Ceiling*, published by the Fikra Foundation, Egypt 2015. He has had several stories and articles published in local and Arab newspapers and magazines. He has won several Yemeni and regional awards for writing, the latest of which is the Al-Rabadi Award for Short Story for the *American Yemeni Newspaper*.

Abdoo Taj is a Yemeni writer who has been published in online magazines such as *Cinema Meem* and *Jeem*. His story 'Borrowing a Head' won first place in the al-Rabadi Award for Short Stories for 2022/2023. His story, 'Sana'a is a Smart and Sustainable City' was part of the anthology *Time Capsule* which was commissioned by the Goethe Institute.

About the Translators

Maisa Almanasreh is a Palestinian translator based in Portugal. She has an MA in Interpreting and Translation from Leeds University and has previously translated fiction for *Egypt + 100: Stories from a Century After Tahrir* (Comma, 2024).

Raph Cormack is a translator and researcher in modern Arabic literature, and author of *Midnight in Cairo: The Female Stars of Egypt's Roaring `20s* (Saqi, 2021) and the forthcoming *Holy Men of the Electronic Age: A Forgotten History of the Occult* (Hurst, 2025). He is Assistant Professor in the Arabic Department at the University of Durham and is an editor of *The Book of Khartoum* and *The Book of Cairo* (both Comma, 2016 and 2019).

Basma Ghalayini is a translator from Gaza whose previous translations have been published by Commonwealth Writers, Deep Vellum Press and Comma Press (*Banthology, The Book of Cairo, The Book of Ramallah* and others). She is the editor of *Palestine + 100: Stories from a Century After the Nakba* (Comma, 2019).

Mohammed Ghalayini worked for two years as a reporter for New York-based Free Speech Radio News in Gaza and as a presenter on the Palestine Satellite Channel. His translations have appeared in *The Book of Khartoum, Palestine + 100, The Book of Ramallah,* and *Egypt + 100* (all with Comma). He works as an air quality scientist and, in late, 2023 offered extensive firsthand reporting on the genocide being conducted in Gaza.

Christiaan James is a diplomat and translator and formerly Director of Public Affairs for the U.S. Embassy in Yemen. He has translated three novels (all with Dar Arab): Ali Al-Muqri's *Adeni Incense* (2023), Mohammed AlAjmi's *The Secret of the Morisco* (2024), and Badr Ahmed's *Five Days Untold* (2021).

Laura Kasinof (editor) is a freelance print journalist, author and documentary filmmaker. She is a former *New York Times* Yemen correspondent and has worked in and around the country since 2009. She is the author of *Don't Be Afraid of the Bullets: An Accidental War Correspondent in Yemen* (Arcade, 2014) and her reporting has appeared in *Slate, Harper's, the Atlantic, Guernica, Virginia Quarterly Review* and many more publications. Laura is currently working on a biography of former Yemen President Ali Abdullah Saleh, forthcoming from Reaktion Books.

Talei Lakeland is a translator from Arabic, German and French into English. She holds an MSc in Arabic-English translation from Heriot-Watt University (2015), having also studied Arabic in Damascus, Brussels and Graz. Born and raised in Cornwall, she has spent over a decade in Germany and Austria, and now lives and works in Bonn.

Andrew Leber is an assistant professor at Tulane University's Department of Political Science, where he researches the politics of the Middle East and North Africa. His translations have appeared in outlets such as *AGNI* online, the *New Statesman*, the *Brooklyn Rail, Jadaliyya* and *Guernica*.

Majd Abu Shawish is a former runner-up in Comma's Emerging Translator Award, with translations in *The Guardian* and two previous and forthcoming Comma titles.

Katherine Van de Vate has previously served as a U.S. diplomat in the Middle East and a curator at the British Library. Her literary translations from Arabic have appeared in *Words Without Borders, Asymptote, ArabLit Quarterly, Y'allah*, and *Sekka*. She is the translator of Badriyah Al Badri's novel *The Last Crossing* (2024).

Special Thanks

The editor would like to thank Mohammed al-Ghobary and Abdallah Siraj for their help. The publisher would like to thank Taher Qassim, Anne Thwaite and everyone at the Liverpool Arab Arts Festival, as well as Su Annagib.

READING THE CITY (IN TRANSLATION)

The Book of Barcelona
Edited by Zoe Turner & Manel Ollé

The Book of Beijing
Edited by Bingbing Li

The Book of Cairo
Edited by Raph Cormack

The Book of Dhaka
Edited by Arunava Sinha & Pushpita Alam

The Book of Gaza
Edited by Atef Abu Saif

The Book of Havana
Edited by Orsola Casagrande

The Book of Istanbul
Edited by Jim Hinks & Gul Turner

The Book of Jakarta
Edited by Maesy Ang & Teddy W. Kusuma

The Book of Khartoum
Edited by Raph Cormack & Max Shmookler

The Book of Prague
Edited by Jim Hinks & Gul Turner

The Book of Riga
Edited by Becca Parkinson & Eva Eglaja-Kristsone

The Book of Rio
Edited by Toni Marques & Katie Slade

The Book of Ramallah
Edited by Maya Abu Al-Hayet

The Book of Reykjavik
Edited by Becca Parkinson & Vera Juliusdottir

ALSO AVAILABLE IN THIS SERIES

The Book of Shanghai
Edited by Dai Congrong & Dr Jin Li

The Book of Tbilisi
Edited by Becca Parkinson & Gvantsa Jobava

The Book of Tehran
Edited by Fereshteh Ahmadi

The Book of Tokyo
Edited by Jim Hinks, Masashi Matsuie
& Michael Emmerich

The Book of Venice
Edited by Orsola Casagrande

READING THE CITY (UK)

The Book of Bristol
Edited by Heather Marks & Joe Melia

The Book of Coventry
Edited by Raef Boylan

The Book of Birmingham
Edited by Khavita Bhanot

The Book of Leeds
Edited by Tom Palmer & Maria Crossan

The Book of Liverpool
Edited by Maria Crossan & Eleanor Rees

The Book of Manchester
Edited by David Sue

The Book of Newcastle
Edited by Zoe Turner & Angela Readman

The Book of Sheffield
Edited by Catherine Taylor

ALSO AVAILABLE FROM COMMA

FUTURES' PAST

Egypt + 100
Stories from a Century After Tahrir
Edited by Ahmed Naji

Iraq + 100
Stories from a Century After the Invasion
Edited by Hassan Blasim

Iran + 100
Stories from a Century After the Coup
Edited by Fereshteh Ahmadi, Rebecca Zahabi
& Peter Behravesh

Kurdistan + 100
Stories from a Future Republic
Edited by Orsola Casagrande & Mustafa Gundogdu

Palestine + 100
Stories from a Century After the Nakba
Edited by Basma Ghalayini